CURVY 13

A BLACK LABEL NOVELLA

NICCI HARRIS

INKI PUBLISHING

CURVY 13

ISBN ebook: 978-1-922492-28-9

ISBN print: 978-1-922492-30-2

Edited by Mostert-Seed Editing

www.mostertseedediting.com

Internal graphics by Nicci Harris

Cover design by Nicci Harris

ALSO BY NICCI HARRIS

The Kids of The District

Facing Us

Our Thing

Cosa Nostra

Her Way

His Pretty Little Burden

His Pretty Little Queen

Their Broken Legend

Black Label Nicci Harris

CurVy 13

CurVy Forever

BLURB

HE CALLS ME PUP,

AND WANTS ME TO PLAY FETCH.

I'm Vallie, but BookTok knows me as @CurvyandBooked.
Dark Romance is my jam, peanut butter, and marmalade.
Mafia. Bully. Why Choose. You name it, and I want to sit in my
beanbag with my battery-operated boyfriend and read it.
Look, if I don't need a chöochie ice bath after a romance, was it even a
love story?
If someone didn't bleed for looking at her, was the hero really that
into her?
But it's just fiction.
Until it's not.
So, when I find a masked man in my living room skimming my
favourite romance novel, all my dark desires become very real
nightmares.
And he is not alone. He has a mentally deranged brother who wants to
play house with me.

Soon, I'm torn between right and wrong, good and bad, and who needs saving from whom...

.

.

.

DISCLAIMER: Nicci never thought she would want to use a pen name until she wrote this absolute insanity. From this book, she has created her Nicci Harris, Black Label, brand. This is pure filth, with minimal plot, and features unhinged male main characters with mummy issues. Caution: the leading characters engage in questionable consent, and the narrative includes depictions of childhood trauma.

For the dark romance girlies who want the 3 Ms— masks, muscles, and monster-sized cocks. And to have their pussy played with the precision of a concert pianist…

This one is for you.

T.W

This is a Nicci Harris Black Label book.

This means it is pure filth, with minimal plot, and features unhinged male main characters with mummy issues.

Caution: the leading characters engage in questionable consent, and the narrative includes depictions of trauma from childhood.

Please visit my website for a detailed list tr!ggers:
<u>HERE</u>

If you prefer a slow burn, plot and spice in equal measure, try Nicci's Kids of The District series and meet the notorious Butcher Boys.

CHAPTER 1

DONNIE

Rain pelts down, creating a curtain of water around my parked SUV. It's white noise, a perpetual sound that relaxes me into the dark depths of the vehicle.

I hit play again.

Her post has seventy-six thousand views—I account for at least a few hundred of them.

I like watching her.

And it is her.

Valentina Relli. The girl on my brother's jury who happened to be sighted by a fan walking into the courthouse this morning. Then leaving at four; a full day's work.

I wasn't sure it was her, but after finding her P.O. Box on her TikTok account, paying the depot a visit with a lot of money and a bribe hard to deny, the receptionist handed over her mail with a new address plate.

The rest is history.

She left court a few hours ago, but she's still not home, so until I see her car pull into the house across the street from where I am parked, I'll watch her posts.

She is entertaining.

Too damn sexy.

I sigh roughly when she bounces in place, singing a Taylor Swift song and showing off her bookcase. I have already noted the window behind her, a narrow sliding window that she leaves cracked open slightly.

Her black #curvyandbooked tank top hides nothing, not because she's trying to be seductive, but because her ample curves stretch the fabric, highlighting her best parts.

She's all woman.

Our Curvy 13.

Long, lush blonde hair that waves down over the full mounds of her chest, the tips dangling an inch from the lower bow, like nipple tassels.

She's not a natural blonde; the dark eyebrows that arch with animation and the lashes that fan each soft cheek are evidence of that.

Her eyes are deep brown, sultry, inset and match her brows and lashes. She is tanned, too.

One look at her, and I can tell she has no idea how beautiful she is, which is a benefit to me. I'm an arrogant arse, and I've never enjoyed the company of anyone like me.

Headlights suddenly filter through the dark.

I lean back into the shadowy pocket of the driver's seat, watching the approaching car slow down, stop, and idle outside her house.

Through their window, I can make out her face, her expression sharp with displeasure, her mouth frantically moving.

She's pissed off.

Beside her a man cast in shadows retaliates, thumping the dashboard and steering wheel like a two-hundred-pound child having a temper tantrum.

She kicks open the passenger door, her foot reaching for the ground, when he grabs her arm. I pause, feeling my impatience heat my muscles.

Calm.

She'll be mine to play with soon enough.

She wrestles with his hold, putting up a hell of a fight that only sets that heat to a boil, knowing I'll be rolling around with that body, pinning it down, feeling it resist...

Not long.

I shuffle to the feral images in my mind.

She gets free from him and storms inside, the rain coating her clothes, weighing them down, her hair sticking to her back and over the mounds of tits, her black eyeliner twin streams rushing over each plush cheek.

Two-hundred-pound dipshit is striding after her when she pushes the door open, turns, and slams it in his face. I almost crack a smile.

He thumps on the wood, hard.

Popcorn would be nice.

I look down at my phone, drawn to her laughter and hollering through the speaker. "I don't even have pearls, but, girl, if I did, chapter six would've had me clutching them and simultaneously wishing for a different kind around my neck."

I cock an eyebrow at her blatant admission, giving so much of herself away for strangers' entertainment.

Finding her the perfect mix of theatrical and innocent, I go to the comments to see what others think about her, a slow grin stretching my lips out as I read.

That chapter got me good!

I needed a coochie ice bath after that one!

Wait until you get to chapter nine!

They adore her.

Wait...

Eww, get off my TikTok.

What is wrong with this girl?

She's obviously lonely.

I hit the sleep button and wait in the dark of the car for her boyfriend to give up and return to his beat-up Honda. The heavy thud of his driver's door pulses through my heart like a starting gun firing.

Not long now.

After watching countless reels on her TikTok account, my cock is already hard and making the decisions for me. I look down, the bulging muscle beating upward beneath my jeans.

I groan.

She is my type, an outward layer of flamboyance, confidence, and humour, that I plan on stripping away to expose her juicy vulnerable insides.

I plan to show her what living inside one of her dark romance novels is like.

Let's see if she likes it there.

———

It's been ten minutes, there is a gap in the rain, and my cock can't wait any longer.

I step from the car, my boots pressing into the muddied water, but I'm not concerned about staying clean. I'll have her so dirty, so defiled, and too afraid to speak up.

As I said, arrogant arse.

I approach the building.

The thing about houses built in the 1970s, like this brick home in front of me, is they all have sliding windows that push inward.

I stalk around the house, past a rose bush in full bloom. The scent carries a feminine note that makes me consider picking one for her.

A nice touch… not my style, though.

Still, I rip a long vine from the bush. Approaching the window in slow strides, I crush a defiant rose that clings to the stem, grinning as the plush petals crumble from the bud, a manifestation of what I'll do to her.

To stress her compliance.

Keeping hold of them and the vine, I use my free hand to shimmy the window, lift it from the groove, twist and fold, and — It comes free.

I catch it before it falls.

The window slides slowly to the floor.

Turning sideways, I duck in through the narrow window and find myself in the centre of her TikTok stage.

The space is dim, but for the fairy lights that decorate her white bookcases illuminating her books—her treasures.

Overhead, the pipes groan with passing water. I anticipated she would shower—arrogance is commonly the result of always being right.

I sprinkle the crushed rose as I stalk the space, the mashed petals marking my path. Stopping beside her bookcase, I trail my tattooed fingers over the spines.

"Eeny, meeny, miny, moe," I mutter darkly before stopping on the smooth surface of a glossy red book.

Pulling it from the stack, I lay the vine between the outer books. I can't stifle my chuckle when little tabs appear like a calling card from her darkest desires.

While I am certain she enjoys the romantic elements—all women do—my ego tells me she has annotated the parts that make her pussy weep and clench.

I flip to a dark purple tab, and a steady grin moves across my lips, and it promises filth.

Fuck.

Achingly hard, I palm my cock as I read one of her favourite scenes. Words wouldn't usually affect me like this, but they aren't words.

They aren't stories.

They are plans.

5

CHAPTER 2

VALLIE

I'm so sick of him.

"Then why do you keep going back to him?" I say to myself. "Because, Vallie, you were in love with him." I scoff at myself. "Was not."

Well, it's over now.

For good this time!

Shutting the shower faucet off, I invoke another groan from the pipes as they protest the one fucking job they have. Just one. The ebb and flow of water.

One job!

Rolling my eyes, I mutter, "You need to get that fixed."

I retort, "No, *you* need to get that fixed."

Oh my God, I wish I had a housemate.

I step from the shower. The free-standing bucket lamps I have set up around the unit and the candles I lit for myself filter through the dark and allow me to see without the intrusive clarity of the overhead strip lights.

Those bastards show every dimple.

I sigh; it's been *a* day.

Grabbing a bright pink towel, I quickly wrap it around my body and tuck an end between my cleavage.

As I walk from the bathroom, something catches my eye. I peer through my open bedroom door and frown.

On the floor at the end of the corridor are small red specks. They rock a little, move even. Like feathers.

Did Oliver get in here?

Is this one of his sick jokes?

My spider sense stirs, prickles—it fucking starts to weave.

I freeze, a whimper shuddering inside my throat. "Hello?"

Really?

Hello?

My steps are slow as I walk towards the small speck on the floor, controlling my breathing, fisting my towel high.

Outside, the rain has stopped but the wind rocks the trees, their limbs brushing my tin roof.

Upon the mysterious fleck, I poke the tiny thing with my big toe, feeling a waxy discharge. It's a rose petal.

The sound of a match dragging along coarse paper filters through the stirring storm. It's close. Inside. My heart races. Someone is behind me.

I'm frozen, my eyes wide on the rose petal. I can't convince myself to move as I listen to a sharp inhale and then a long exhale so deep it could be coming from Hell.

"It's in your head," I say to myself.

"Not this time." A voice that rivals the depth of the breath soars towards me.

I fly around to find a dark figure, a broad, very clearly male silhouette. *I can't speak.*

The ember flares as he draws another breath in, a glittering red dot within an eerie dark outline.

"I hope you don't mind me using the matches. I found them on your bookcase—'I burn for book boyfriends.' Unique merchandise. Sorry to open it, but I like using matches. Always thought that a cigarette tastes better with that sulphur residue filtering through it."

He lowers the cigarette and takes a step forward. "Or maybe it just reminds me of my youth."

Another step.

But I still can't move.

The edge of the bookcase slides past him, the shadow it created slipping away. The glow of the fairy lights touches the side of his face, and I can see more of him.

All the terror inside me rises.

The side of his head is smooth and shiny, and it takes me a moment to realise he's wearing a metallic mask, one plucked straight from a drama theatre; lips curved down to create an elaborate sad expression; dual holes hollowed to allow the gloss of two real eyes to peer through.

The mask slowly tilts.

Well, fuck, that's unnerving.

I step backwards quickly, my back crashing into the front door. The door I should open, should run through. A door, a front door—oh *God*. But my hands, my stupid locked hands shake, and my mind idles on controlling them.

Open the door! Run!

"I wouldn't do that," he warns, reading my thoughts or anticipating my next move, I don't know which.

He's done this before?

Will he kill me?

"What do you want?" Finally, my mouth catches up, but my hands are still stalling in that place of shock.

"I want to help you with your TikToks."

What?

My head spins, and suddenly, I'm in a vacuum, the room rotating around me, faster and faster and faster. I grip the wall. Stare at the ground. Try to remain upright. "What?"

He takes another step, and the world was reeling around, circling me, halts as he emerges.

I take him in. A black boot comes into view, the mud and dirt a film beneath it.

Up.

A long denim-covered leg, thick thigh, and black belt with a chrome buckle.

I should remember these things.

Up.

Protruding muscles rise and shift beneath a dark shirt.

Then, a full view of the mask.

This has to be a joke.

He works out.

He's a stripper or an actor…

What would he want with me?

Not a time for your sensitivities, Vallie.

"Is this a joke?" My voice trembles along the length of each word. "Did Oliver send you? As a way to humiliate me? Or…" *I know it's crazy.*

Oliver wouldn't do this.

He slowly lifts his hand, achingly slow, and his tattooed thumb swipes across a phone, activating the screen where the image of me sinks harrowing dread into the pit of my stomach. That was the day I begged a masked man to kidnap me—when I *joked* about it.

My body catches up.

Shocked into action, I turn to get the door open, tugging on it hard.

This is happening.

This is real.

It swings, opens, and then crashes to a thundering close. It bangs so hard that the decorative glass pieces rattle, and, *God*, I hope someone outside hears.

But it's dark and stormy.

This is a sleepy neighbourhood.

Sleepy people fucking sleep!

So, I cower and brace my hands over my head, but nothing

comes. Yet I know he is right behind me.

Hovering over me.

The press of his presence at my back becomes all I can feel. My breath slows for long moments that stretch and engulf me, fear and a strange kind of thrill, too.

Endorphins, like being high.

With a hand pressed to the door on either side of my shoulders, his breath on my spine, his formidable energy is as tangible as any touch.

"Now, I have a filleting knife in my boot. I don't want to use it. I don't even want to grab it. It'll slide so quickly into your soft skin that you'll probably miss it. Until your blood roars through your veins as it drains from you. So, behave and listen," he says, his voice close, deep, and somehow capable of purring seductively against my inner ears. "No one has to get hurt. Here is one for your dark romance stories... Did you know they used to lobotomise women in the dark ages, so they had living dolls? See, they would just lay there after that, warm bodies, strong heartbeat, wet cunt, obedient but better still, giddy and fun."

I start to sob.

"Easy." He spins me to face him, cupping my cheeks and cradling my weak head. "Calm." My body wants to drop to the floor, my survival instincts cowering to his vile comment. "I won't be doing that to you. I want you to know what I'm capable of. What I'll do if I have to."

He lifts me effortlessly into his thick, strong arms, and I just let him. I just fucking *let* him. Let the helplessness render me nothing but compliant in this moment.

"I think you're going to do as you're told without the screwdriver through your eye. Am I right?"

I nod.

"Very good, Thirteen."

Thirteen?

Why did he—

Oh God. I've been called thirteen all day. *Dammit;* the

connection almost slips through without me noticing, almost lost importance, choked by my fear.

Thirteen.

My juror number.

This morning, my first day of compulsory jury service, I was given a number for privacy. A numeral instead of a name; that is the way it works.

I store that information. *This is good.* It brings me hope. This isn't a random killing. He's linked somehow to the case I am part of. *Think, Vallie.*

Think.

A little girl was kidnapped.

She was found with a thirty-four-year-old man.

He had her for less than three hours.

The mother is pressing charges.

When he lowers me to my reading beanbag—covered in cupcakes like a damn little girl's—I grip the towel as it slides, but he takes a fist full.

My pulse hits the back of my throat, my previous hope sinking as he rips the towel from my body.

I gasp, tears bursting from my eyes, mingling with my fitful pleas. "No. Please." I throw my arms across my body.

"No clothes for you. Isn't that the way this goes?"

The way what goes?

I don't understand.

To humiliate me?

"This game is going to play out a little differently to the usual, 'you run and if I catch you, yada, yada.'"

Two eyes, deeply set into metallic hollows, roam my body. I can't see his expression but feel heat deep inside my tissue. A burn from embarrassment. The scorching of being debased. I won't let it win.

"Instead of you running and me hunting you," he says, amusement dripping from his deep tone. "I'm going to switch the lights off and stalk around in the shadows. If you can get to

12

your phone, I will let you use it, but if I get to it first, I'm going to pin you down and fuck you to the most terrifying orgasm of your life. You'll cry and come, hate it and love it."

I can't hear him, drowning in the fact I'm nude, confused by *thirteen*, reeling over all the details I should memorise for when I get to my phone.

Dark belt buckle.

Tattooed fingers.

Six-four-ish, maybe.

With all my body exposed to him, my insecurities snatch my attention again.

I don't even let Oliver see me completely naked unless I'm lying under him. Lights off. That's the only way I can come, the only way I can enjoy myself. Not that I'll enjoy myself…

This isn't a game.

This isn't fun.

Lesson learned.

He is suddenly low in front of me, a metal mask prowling up my body.

"Did you hear me?" I can see his lips through the wide, sad curve. They are the only thing human about him. I imagine they'll be the only soft thing, too.

What? Shut the fuck up.

Nothing is soft.

I recoil into the beanbag, wishing to disappear as his encroaching body hovers over mine. His two glossy eyes sweep over me again, my arms knotted around my torso, hiding as much as possible.

Then he pulls his phone out and snaps a picture of me.

I gasp in horror. "No!"

He buries his phone in his back pocket and leans in a little closer, his breath rushing through the gap in the mask. "What's wrong?"

"Don't share that."

"Never. That's for me." He hums through a pause. "You need

a pet name. All the heroines in your dark romance books have pet names. What was the one I just read? Kitten? I like it, but it's not you. Plus, I don't like cats. How about pup? My sweet, excitable, rolling little pup. It matches the flamboyant girl from your TikTok. The self-assured and sassy one who bounces her sweet tits around for strangers. Wanting to be praised. Wanting a belly rub."

"I don't like it."

"I don't care."

Play cool.

Run out the front door.

When you can, run.

Naked?

You're fucking naked!

"I get my phone, and you leave?"

"Enough questions." He rises to his full height; the thick column of his erection is in line with my gaze. He rubs it and groans. "Playtime starts now, Pup."

It is quick.

He takes two paces to the bookcase and readies one hand on the clicker for the fairy lights and one on the switch for the freestanding lamp.

My eyes widen, breath bated, waiting, pulse hammering in my throat like a drum counting down.

One.

Two.

Three…

Click.

Light melts to pitch black.

"Go fetch your phone."

CHAPTER 3

DONNIE

I switched the lights off for her.

I'm not a complete bastard. It appears my Curvy Thirteen isn't as confident as she seems behind the screen. I'll have to work on that over the next four days while I use her body in every way she's ever dreamed about, twisting her dark desires into a nightmarish reality.

I still and listen.

The beans in the bag shuffle, and I snap my head towards the sound. Footsteps slide across the floor in an even and cautious way. It's adorable.

I hear her exhale a long, shaky breath.

It's a pity I can't see her luscious body, but it's burned into my damn memory. Thick thighs that touch at the top, smooth knees—I've always liked smooth knees. Her legs narrow in a lovely way to small ankles and cute feet, bright pink nail polish. I want to suck that pink colour into my mouth while I fold all that woman in half.

Her stomach is round and supple, and her waist is smaller—

like she's wearing a fucking corset—before spilling out again with heavy tits I could get lost in.

Shaking the vision away, I hone my senses back to my Pup as she tries to sneak around the room. I move like a wraith towards the door, and her steps fumble.

I reach behind my head and tug my shirt off; I freeze and listen, then throw it in her direction.

She whimpers.

Got her.

I used to play laser tag with my brothers when I was young, unmatched in the dark light challenge.

This is far more fun.

She is in the hallway now.

My steps are confident and even as I follow her up the dark hall, sensing she is close. I step on something that crunches under my shoe, and her steps take off, yelps of pure panic and adrenaline sailing.

Goddamn—her panic. Arousal throbs through me like a fucking stubbed toe.

I rip my belt off, the sound of it slicing through the loop and lashing out cracks through the air.

I stop just shy of the bedroom, flanked by darkness. I casually lean down and slide my boots off, unbutton my jeans, drop them and my briefs to the floor.

Straightening, I follow her into her room.

I have to have her.

In only my mask, my cock thumping at my navel, I corner my Pup in her room. She is frantic, fumbling around the dresser in the dark, blind fingers searching the last place she saw her phone.

But it's not there.

She starts to sob.

She knows.

I already have it.

Never said I play fair, but that's not the point.

I snatch the nape of her neck and toss her to the bed, pin her to the mattress and lay my body over hers.

"Let me go!"

Goddamn.

"I'll do anything."

She thrashes around.

Feeling her soft flesh against my own draws precum from my balls. It smears her lower back as I grind against her, feeling a frenzy of need.

"Hush, Pup." I reach around her body, between her legs, and swipe two fingers through her pussy, finding the hairless, plump flesh already dripping.

I groan. "*Fuck.* You *do* want this. It's not an act for your followers. You can't help yourself. Mmm. Feel that... Fuck. So smooth and wet."

She shakes from head to toe.

A cry breaches the room—finally—her pride plummets, her insecure demons no longer prevailing. Instead, a lovely air of terror mixes with pure, abandoned lust.

"Are you going to kill me?" She gyrates beneath me—*fuuuck.* "After *this*? Are you going to kill me?"

"I don't want to." My voice lowers, my breath beating off the skin on her back, lifting her clean scent towards me. I play along her folds, dipping a finger in and out, too quick for her to latch on to. "So slippery. That's a good girl. Keep dripping for me. Such a desperate little thing. Greedy for attention. From your followers, and from *me*."

Meshed with her body, I make sure she feels every inch of me. No space between us; I couldn't bear it now.

I push two fingers into her, and she freezes.

"Don't," I warn darkly. "Don't do that. Don't pretend. You know that you want to hold my fingers. Suck them in. I like to battle with these muscles."

She sobs into the mattress.

"Wider for me. I don't just shove my fingers into a woman,

Pup. I work and explore, massage along each surface, stimulate every muscle." Her legs widen. "*Yes*. Damn, your pussy is soft."

I rub my erection through the seam of her arse cheeks while I study her insides.

She is burning hot.

Thick and tight.

Then, I feel a flutter from her, a response to my penetration that she can't quell, so I scoop and hit that spot.

She moans, and I smile.

Her temperature spikes again, dread, adrenaline, fear, and arousal boiling her up. "God, you're warm."

I tilt my hips, dragging my cock down to where my fingers play. Slowly, I slide both digits out, touching and scissoring to spread her and get her ready.

I nudge my cock into the outer layer of her pussy. She sobs words into the mattress. Incoherent words. "What's that?"

She gasps for air as she says, "Condom."

"Hell no."

"*Please.*"

I know she's not going to get pregnant, compliments of another TikTok where she flashes the contraceptive implant in her arm. So, my answer is an aggressive thrust into her warm, wet depths.

She screams as I invade her snug flesh, and my cock thickens to the point of absolute agony.

She fights against me, but that only frees her pussy from the clutches of her restraint. Her body mewls in defiance while her insides lock hard.

"*Yes.* That's my good girl. *Fuck*, you're strong." I pant, my head swimming already. "*Like that.* Choke this big cock. Strangle it like you hate it. A stranger. Enjoying you… Obsessing. Over. You. *Fuck. Yes.*" I hammer into her. "This was just gonna be four days. So I can control you during the trial but this pussy could become very addictive."

My mouth waters as I fuck her.

I pull my fingers from between her legs and swallow them. A mouthful of liquid silk hits my tongue, her perfect, clean, salty essence.

Pinning her under the weight of my much larger, far stronger body, I fuck her and taste her and lose my mind.

"You hold me so good. A tight little hole made for me," I barely get the words out. "You want me deeper. Do you? *Yes.* You do. You want me deep, Pup. So deep you're not sure you'll survive."

She shakes her head with fierce adamance, her arse jiggling against my thrusts. I groan as her body screams the primal truth loud and fucking clear.

She pumps me with her pussy.

Humming around her satin juices, I reluctantly pop my fingers out and reach around to bear down on her clit.

Her legs convulse.

She *will* come all over my cock whether she wants to or not.

Deep laughter leaves me. "This is clearly not your body tonight, Pup. It's mine. It obeys me."

She shudders and cries out, entirely at my mercy, batted with need and blind with the desire to climax.

"That's it. That's… That's it. Milk my cock. Suck it out of me."

Heat belts me hard.

A gruff sound tears up my throat as my balls pulse and fire. I pinch her fat, little clit and thrust so deep, so hard, the sensitive crown of my cock smashes her cervix.

I come inside her, hard and violently, and she drains me through her own orgasm, whimpers of defeat wrestling with her moans of dark pleasure.

CHAPTER 4

TYLER

My hand is down the front of my jeans, my cock a slick, hard rod in my working fist. The perfectly placed keys of Widor on piano play in my mind like he is hitting the ivories beside me as I rub my cock.

But then *her* name carves into my mind, the name that haunts me, torments me—*Martha Argerich*.

Fuck!

Not that bitch.

I release my cock.

I'm leaning beside her front door in a pocket of darkness. The sounds of my brother fucking, slapping, and grunting, a building symphony, have just stopped, and so has Widor playing piano in A Minor.

Martha Argerich ruins everything.

I tug my hand out.

Like fuck he was getting all the playtime with her. Hell, I've seen her. Watched her Instagram and TikTok more times than I can count—jerked off in equal count.

The moment she giggled at her own filthy joke, I was a damn

goner. Her giggle was in a mezzo-soprano, reminiscent of the tinkling sound of the piano's upper register until it built to a full-blown cascade of arpeggios.

It blew my mind.

I blew my load on my phone.

The memory of my piano teacher's snarl hits my forehead. *"Tyler, your hand is always down your damn pants. Dirty boys can't play piano."*

Yeah, *bitch*, I like to look at you.

I like to touch myself while I do.

Fuck, women.

I like them too much.

It's just the way I'm tuned.

Fuck her!

My leg twitches to kick the door down, but that would be dumb, and I swore to my brothers that I wouldn't be dumb today. Not today.

I inhale calming, melodic thoughts: big tits in my face, fat nipple between my teeth, engulfed in soft arms that rock me, a sweet hum that flows like *Für Elise*...

My cock stirs against my zipper.

I exhale the bitch who called me a pervert just because I mentioned wanting to be posed with her when they buried us together. I wanted my cock to be put inside her so we would be connected until we crumbled to pieces of earth.

That's not perverted.

It's romantic, dammit!

I exhale that bitch.

That's better.

A grin plays on my lips when I test the front door. It turns with ease, the gate to heaven swinging slowly inward, revealing pitch black.

"Easy, Pup," I hear my brother's deep voice, a bass tone, cooing to her as she sobs, and it bothers me instantly.

I step inside, close access to her, lock it tight, and try to flick the excitement from my fingers, not wanting to scare her, freak her out—

"You're a freak."

"Shut up!" I snap to her phantom.

"Tyler?" My brother's authoritarian timbre drifts down the corridor. "Come here and meet our puppy."

"A puppy?" I grin. "I always wanted a puppy."

Retrieving my phone from my back pocket, I swipe the torch on, a guiding light to her, illuminating a narrow passage.

I walk down the hall, led by the glow. I stop beside an open door, directing the torch until it spotlights a beautiful blonde unable to move from her place bent over the mattress. She is naked. Wet.

A blush mars her skin.

Shit.

It's happening again.

My heart starts to hurt; the beat is fast but rhythmic as my eyes sweep over her wondrously, memorising, hypnotised by all that luscious flesh— I'm falling in love.

"Cut that out," Donnie warns me, fisting her hair, lifting her head off the bed as if to present a prize catch. The bite at her scalp tears a yelp from her—soprano notes that don't seem to suit her soft, smooth form.

No.

Dropping the phone, I lunge forward. The torch lands upward, a strobe of light my body cuts through.

I shove him away from her, but she screams, a pitch for pain, as strands of her hair rip out, remaining in his fist.

"Sorry, baby." I collect her into my arms, and she trembles hard. My heart soars. "I got you."

"Goddammit!" Donnie barks. "I told you to take your damn medication this morning."

"Ignore him," I say, nuzzling into her blonde hair. She is sobbing hard; her cheeks are wet and pink and it's as though she's broken.

Have to fix her.

"Where is your damn mask?"

Oh yeah, the mask.

Fuck it.

I stride to the bedroom door and use my elbow to flick the light switch on the wall. With her—a soft, warm body cradled against mine—I take her away from him. "Donnie isn't very nice sometimes, but he looks after us," I admit. "He'll look after you, too."

Using my elbow again, I knock the switch. A bright strip light bursts the bathroom into clarity.

My pulse is racing as I set her down on the tiles in the shower and turn it on. Arranging the faucet, I angle it so the stream slides down the wall, pooling around her body and creating puddles of water I can use to clean her.

But she doesn't move.

She's in shock. Her legs flop apart. Her palms protect her pretty face, sobs violently crash into them.

The broken weeping makes her shake, the sound a clashing of painful chest notes.

I look her over.

Straightaway, I see my brother's cum sliding from between her puffy pussy lips.

I scoop it out, and she freezes, the sad sobbing melody petrified to silence as she becomes a statue.

"No, no, baby. I won't hurt you. I was just cleaning you up." I am so fucking hard, my cock feels as though it will pop like warm champagne, but I'll control myself.

I push two fingers into her and scoop upward, collecting the mess from her. She's warm, *so* warm, so wanting, responsive —*fuck*. I realise I'm fingering her now, and she lowers her hands to stare at me.

Our eyes meet.

"Hi," I breathe.

And sparks fucking fly between us, an intense and

meaningful melody builds in my ears, and my world tilts, hers does, too. I can tell. "I'm Tyler."

She's gaping at me, still recovering. I get it; Donnie said he needed to scare her, break her, have her question everything, and then we will be in control.

But I'm here now.

And shit... Her irises appear brown in her TikTok clips, but here, with the white tiles and overhead strip lighting, they are more than brown. Of course, they are. In here, they're glittered in gold.

"Let me wash you," I say. The excitement I feel is a drone I can't escape, but I try to keep my breathing even.

I finger her swollen channel, twisting inside the pulsing flesh, pulling out, missing her, so I enter her again and again.

"This is my brother," Donnie states from the doorway, the distinct sound of inhaling and exhaling, the stoking of his cigarette, interrupting his words. "But he's not the reason we are here. My other brother is. *Dexter Vaughn.* You recognise that name, *Thirteen?*"

She lifts her knees and plants her bare feet on the tiles, offering me a better angle and view. Using the puddle of water that collects around her backside, I splash her pretty lips and finger the clean water into her.

Her head lands on the wall behind her, overcome by my penetration. She closes her eyes, shaking her head.

"Don't fight it. I'll make you orgasm, and you can push my brother's cum out when you do. Maybe, one day, I can replace it with mine. *Yeah? Would you like that?*"

Her eyes snap open and lock onto me. I think that's a *yes.*

I can't read her expression, pinched brows, searching gaze. She looks startled or confused, which I get—I'm confused by what we are feeling, too.

She looks at my mouth, and I realise I'm humming again. It's a sweet, light melody.

"He's a pianist," Donnie advises. "He hums sometimes. Don't make him feel weird about it."

Was.

Was a pianist.

He continues, "We are going to stay here. You are going to show up each day for your jury duty. Sit through the evidence. Pay attention. And when the time comes, you will vote for a not-guilty verdict."

He pauses, the silence a message. "Because if my brother goes to prison for kidnapping that stupid little girl, I'll still be here. Tyler will still be here. And we'll be with you. This five-day-long engagement will become your life sentence. That's what you always wanted? Isn't it? What you talk about with your followers?"

His words widen her eyes further; *so pretty.*

She clutches at her chest, holding her frantic heart inside as it tries to beat through her flesh.

I can hear it.

I dip and rest my ear over her hand until she moves it away, and my cheek connects with her skin. Her heart—*my heart*—thrashes around. An erratic tempo.

I pull my fingers from inside her and turn to glare a demand at Donnie. *Mine.*

He's leaning on the frame, looking satiated and well fucked, sucking the cigarette as though it's smooth as air, sweet as pussy, oxygen for his dark soul.

"I want her."

Through the metallic mask, I see his eyes blaze, but he cools the flames inside them just as quickly.

"Do you want my brother to look after you?" His voice has an edge, moving around a deep resonance I don't recognise from him. He is usually very impartial, steady, even.

She looks at me, so I nod to encourage the same response. "Go on."

"*Yes.* I want *him* to look after me." Her voice. *Shit.* Her voice is better than through the microphone, a sonata of husky arousal and trembling uncertainty; she's an alto.

Elated, I look at Donnie, who flicks the cigarette to the floor and smashes it hard with his boot. He can't deny me anything. "Fine." The word is almost a punch. "Play with the puppy. I'll go get your meds."

He turns to leave but stops, saying over his shoulder. "If you fuck with Tyler's emotions, I'll make good on that new dark romance scene and shove a screwdriver into your brain, scramble it to doll-like perfection, then I'll let him keep you like that. You understand, Pup?"

The blood leaves her cheeks.

I wouldn't let him do that.

CHAPTER 5

VALLIE

Fucking lunatic.

The bluest eyes I've ever seen stare straight through me, a hummed lullaby leaves an adoring smile, and the utterly psychotic man who possesses both is sliding long tattooed fingers in and out of me.

I have snapped.

My knees are shaking. I suck sharp slices of air in, ignoring the burn, needing the oxygen for clarity.

You're going to be okay.

I inhale deeply and force the air out slowly, gathering a sense of calm I do not truly feel.

I look down between my legs. The deep penetration of his fingers is disturbing, nauseating, and yet, gifts a gentleness my body seems desperate to embrace after being taken so roughly only moments ago.

Using this reprieve, one that seems still, I mentally sort through information.

I've already lost some detail to the shock of the past two

hours: Donnie fucked me. I came, and so did he. Tyler is his fucking unhinged brother, and I have to make sure their other brother, Dexter, gets a not-guilty verdict.

Facts.

Those are the facts.

Details be gone.

"This is so lovely," Tyler murmurs, dragging his tongue along his lower lip, moistening it.

I watch him touch me.

He's not unattractive at all, though I wish he fucking was, but a tanned fallen angel sits with me in the shower. He is in his mid-twenties, with cheeks etched to the sheer lines of a diamond and blue eyes haloed by long dark strands of hair that skate the tops of his shoulders.

He's fucking pretty, and I hate it.

But I know what to do.

I should have Stockholm syndrome—not actually have it, only pretend I do. These guys are clinically psychotic, there is no doubt, but neither seems unintelligent.

So, they'll think I'm conditioned to them, and that they have won. I should act as if I'm falling in love and gain their trust. Try to get a photo or two—evidence. Be patient. I'll wait until I know it's safe, and I'll be prepared. I'll put all three brothers behind bars!

My heart beats strongly as I grip Tyler's tattooed hand. He flinches when my fingers touch his knuckles. For a moment, I feel raised skin, uneven and strange, but I ignore it and focus, guiding his finger into me.

I moan.

He groans.

I lift my hips to meet them and even... allow my body to enjoy it. I'll separate the two pieces of me.

Sever them right now.

There is me.

Then there is my body.

I don't understand this mindset, or whether it's good or bad, but it feels like a survival instinct buried deep. A mother lifting a two-ton car to save a baby… *that kind of thing.*

"Can I taste you, baby?"

Can I do this?

I nod, widening my thighs for him. He is vital to staying alive, fed, and being treated well; I can just feel it. Vulnerability flows from him, but volatility stirs through that force, so I have to keep my cool. Be smart.

As I pull his face down, I thread my finger through his dark hair, pretending there is love in my touch. Even better, if he's between my legs, he can't stare at the rolls of my stomach. I try desperately not to think about being so utterly exposed to him or the parts I twitch to cover.

That won't help my act.

He manoeuvres quickly, kneeling, able to get down on his elbows and press his face between my thighs. His jeans and the sleeves of his black shirt are already damp from the water pooling on the shower floor.

With his fingers still inside me, his lips meet my pussy and suck with not an inkling of hesitation. I hate it, but it's a nice change from Oliver's one-lick attempts.

He gently frenches my pussy with a skilled tongue and mouth, but even if he were an amateur, the playful eagerness in his motion is enough to send me into a spin.

I stroke his hair when he uses his tongue to lap at the clean juices being drawn from me by his fingers.

A moan tumbles through my lips as the primitive sensation climbs from his working fingers and lapping tongue up my spine, a long, slow building of something out of my control.

But that's okay, Vallie.

This is your body.

Not your mind.

They'll never have your mind.

"A contralto," he murmurs into my pussy, before sliding his finger out to feed his tongue more of my juices.

Donnie said he was a pianist.

Even though it's partly water leaking from me, my juices mingle in that clear liquid, and he seems dehydrated as fuck. And he's coming off more like Beethoven the dog than Beethoven, one of the greatest composers.

"I'll make you a soprano, baby."

He rotates his hand so his fingers twist inside me, his thumb angled down and edging between my arse cheeks.

Squeezing the dark strands on his crown, enough to burn his scalp with my defiance, fear, resistance, and uncertainty, I make my feelings known but don't stop him.

I don't stop him when he uses the fluid from my pussy to massage around that new place, or when he uses his wide shoulders to push my thighs further apart.

I don't say a word when he edges an entire thick thumb into my puckering hole or starts to fuck me in both places. But I can't quell the throaty cry that breaks through my uncertain lips.

"That's it. You like feeding me your pussy, don't you? You like me taking care of you, baby." He lifts his head and grins, his mouth devilish with child-like wonder, dripping with silky clear juices. "I'm going to be so good to you."

My eyes roll. *Ugh. Crazy motherfucker.* He dips down again and suctions my sensitive clit, and I buck to the pace of his deep, thorough penetration.

That's when the humming starts again, and his fingers and thumb seem orchestrated to the beat. He's playing me; my inner walls, the keys, his humming, the composer.

It's a gentle, soft motion at first, then it intensifies, each movement more pronounced, prouder, demanding.

My pussy ripples. The way he commands the sensation is flawless—harmonious.

Everything tightens. His humming matches the brewing of desire, the rise of heat, the ebb of shame, the need to come.

A skilled pianist can navigate keys to create an unforgettable musical experience, and Tyler is harmonising the penetration into both my holes with a wicked tongue lashing at the end notes.

Then he strikes with full force.

His humming peaks as though he's letting loose on the keys, the play cresting, his fingers fucking me hard, hitting every spot with perfect precision until my entire body seizes, and he pounds the final chord to my high cries.

Stars blanket my vision.

I shudder the sensation out.

It seems to go on and on…

"You're a mezzo-soprano when you climax for me." He licks me softly. "That's the perfect range for your pleasure, baby. Soothing and long."

Reeling, I lift my head and gasp.

Donnie casually stands in the doorway, his long arms stretched up, gripping the overhead frame. His biceps frame the metallic mask, and it's a thing of nightmares.

My breath hitches.

The mask tilts in that eerie way. "Do you like it when my brother licks your pussy, Pup?"

Be smart.

Slowly, with feigned reluctance, I begin to nod. "Yes."

The mask just stares at me.

What the fuck is he thinking?

He knows, Vallie.

He's onto you.

My pulse races. And I feel a stirring between my legs as Tyler licks me softly and Donnie just stares; both press their energy to my skin.

Donnie breaks the moment. "I think you've tasted her enough. We need to feed the puppy, Tyler. *And* she needs a good night's sleep, so no one has any reason to be concerned about her tomorrow when she is a very good little *thirteen*."

Tyler lifts his head and smiles at me as though we are lovers, and this is just another day. "What do you wanna eat, baby? Donnie can cook everything and anything."

Donnie clears his throat.

I arch an eyebrow, not expecting that. I imagined them as monsters who lurk in the dark, kidnapping children and women, but a pianist and a food enthusiast?

I would've never guessed.

Lifting my knees, I band my legs with my arms, cuddle my breasts and tummy, and concentrate on my body for a moment. *I'm okay. You're going to be okay.* "I'll eat—"

"Don't say you'll eat anything," Donnie states, his voice even. "No one eats *everything*."

I look from Tyler's striking yet deranged blue gaze to the metallic plane that covers Donnie's face.

Both fucking unnerving.

"Take the mask off." The words fall through my lips, so I quickly explain. "It's pointless. I know what Tyler looks like and your names. I know *who* you are."

"That is the last time you make a demand." Donnie takes a step forward, a show of power, his body blocking the overhead light. His shadow blankets my legs. "The next one will result in severe punishment."

I recoil; my spine hits the tiles.

Not smart, Vallie.

"You kidnap me, fuck me, and now you want me to have dinner with you?"

"I didn't kidnap you. This is *your* house, Pup. Just think of us as your temporary housemates."

Oh, the irony…

Be careful what you wish for, Vallie.

"Pizza," I spit out.

It's the first thing that comes to mind—a blatant rejection. I hope he gets that. I don't like the idea of Donnie cooking for me. It feels too domestic, too friendly. Too *weird.* But then—I look at

Tyler—I'm going to have to get used to weird if I'm to survive this. "Just get a pizza."

Donnie stills, and *God*, I wish I could see his face. "Pizza and then bed, Pup."

I can feel his grin as it slowly widens; how that can be, I don't know. "I'll be the one tucking you in."

CHAPTER 6

VALLIE

Two eyes stare at me through the metallic mask as he slides the second pizza from the oven, my mitten on his hand, a pink paw-shaped mitten that Oliver bought me.

This is a dream, Vallie.

It's too weird.

I face Tyler at the dining room table. It's only the second time I have ever eaten here. Last time, I had far more clothes on, but this time, I'm in only Tyler's shirt. It hangs to my knees and fits snugly around my breasts.

Tyler is wearing the sleeveless-tee he had on under his shirt. It displays all the lean muscles across his upper chest and shoulders, the kind a professional fighter would have. He's working his way through his pepperoni slice in slow chews, his eyes locked on my breasts squished into his top.

"Where's your family? Why are you all alone? I don't like it," he says around the bite, lifting his gaze to meet mine.

Lunatic! He wants to chat, like this is normal, like we are on a date? A little get-to-know-you? Fuck.

It's hard, but I don't react. "I don't want to talk about my family right now."

"Tough." Donnie joins us at the table, placing the second pizza down. The sight of olives and anchovies turns my stomach. "Tyler asked you a question. Answer him."

I grab a slice and pick the anchovies and olives from the steaming melted cheese. I need to do something with my hands, to hide the way they shake. "They live in another city, and I don't talk to them much."

Tyler says, "Why?"

"What are you doing?" Donnie asks, burning holes into my hand as I rearrange his pizza.

"I'm not really a fan of olives and anchovies."

"I'll eat *anything? Fucksake.* It's classic Italian. They taste like your pussy, and they are fucking *delicious,* just like your pussy." He cocks his head at the slice. "Eat them."

"You eat them!" I spurt out, wanting him to take his damn mask off and be slightly human.

A heavy pause passes between us. "I'll eat later. Eat them. I made this for you, so be polite."

My mouth drops open, and I struggle to hold my tongue this time. "I didn't realise manners were still upheld in hostage-captive situations."

Shut up, Vallie.

"Manners are always upheld."

I look at Tyler as his smirk meets the new pizza slice, his teeth ripping into it, his throat humming a melody around the bite. "It *is* fucking delicious, but your pussy is better."

Exhaling hard, I relent and take a bite of pizza.

The salt from both the anchovies and the olives assaults my tongue and cheeks, drawing saliva from them, then the cheese creates a buttery blanket and...

It's kinda nice.

They both stare at me as I chew, so I offer, "Fine. It *is* quite pleasant." Then I add, "Unlike you two."

They both laugh, deep and gravelly, and it's the most disturbing sound to hear bouncing around my unit only hours after I was debased, humiliated, and threatened. Ice moves through my veins, reaching my cheeks and fingertips.

I don't want to feel normal.

"So," Donnie says, his laughter dwindling. "Back to your family, Pup. Why don't you speak to them."

A hint of agitation laces through his tone as he asks this, but it's strange and hard to figure out. *Is he protective? Does he care? Is he angry? I can't quite tell what it is.*

I just clear the air.

Making me appear more human can only help my cause. It's what the police advise in these situations: be human. Say your name. Mention your loved ones. Make yourself a real person in their eyes and grasp for compassion.

"My mum and dad are deeply religious, heavily conservative, and unwilling to see any opinion other than theirs. That's all." I shrug stiffly. "I don't have an emotional story for you. I'm just a normal girl. No trauma. No poverty. I was raised well, but I don't enjoy my family's company. We are different. And that's fine—"

"And the douchebag from earlier?" Donnie asks, his tone deep with warning.

A shudder rushes up my spine, knowing he has been watching me. "Who?"

"What douchebag from earlier?" Tyler drops his pizza slice. "What douchebag from earlier. Why didn't I kno—"

"Calm down." Donnie watches me eat for a moment; heavy thoughts play in the tilt of his head.

"So," he finally says. "Who is he? Someone we need to concern ourselves with. He might pose a small problem this week. He nearly knocked your door down."

Tyler's fist thumps the table. "He what?"

"Tyler!" Donnie stands. "Stop that right now."

He walks to the kitchen, grabs a glass from the cupboard and fills it with water from the sink. His eyes never leave us; the mask is always directly face-on.

Walking to us, he fists a packet of pills from his jeans. He pops two from the plastic pocket onto the table in front of Tyler and sets the water down.

"Take your damn meds."

"I want to know about the douch—"

"Take the meds!" Donnie growls, and I sink into my chair. The aggressive tone adds weight to my pelvis. Locks me in place. I don't move or speak.

He stalks around the table to me, ducks, grabs my arm and hauls me over his shoulder, where I dangle. My stomach mashes against the hard muscles rippling through his bicep.

I gasp but hold the scream inside. To pull off a kind of Stockholm syndrome, I need to keep my cool.

Donnie squeezes my arse cheek to the point of pain and groans when I whimper. "You take your meds and have a damn nap. I'm putting the puppy to bed. Don't come in. You're not invited, Tyler. Do you understand?"

"But—"

"No buts!" He barks, the sound slicing through the air, not allowing further debate.

He carries me down the hallway to my bedroom, calling, "She's not yours!"

Heat hits the backs of my eyes.

I hope he turns the lights off so I can cry again. I'm not sure I can pretend to fall in love with Donnie.

Not now.

I'm too tired.

It's easy to fool Tyler. His reality is so warped already, but Donnie seems grounded and sceptical.

I want to sleep.

Wake up tomorrow.

It might all be over.

You'll be alone, again...

My heart aches in my chest, under pressure to pump steady when it wants to break free.

CHAPTER 7

VALLIE

Switching the tap on, I just let it run, let it groan.

I stare at my reflection in the mirror, gripping the vanity for balance, finding the view ahead unsettling.

Buried in my eyes are painful emotions. The script I've been playing is only on the surface, and leaking from deep within me is the truth.

The fear…

Uncertainty.

And another thing. One far more concerning—it's nice to be asked about my life, and it's nice to be wanted, lusted after, even. So, while I'm literally defiled, I also feel desired.

Which is sick.

And Tyler.

Fuck him for being so vulnerable; that's my weakness. If there is a damn underdog, I'm on my knees in the dirt, fleas landing on me, so that I can feed it.

I could save him…

I could save him from Donnie.

I cup the water flowing from the tap and splash my face,

washing the evidence of that thought down the drain, where I hope it gets stuck and blows up the old, rusty pipes.

Throwing my matted blonde hair over my shoulder, I shake it to an almost bearable state. I look like shit. I look like I've been kidnapped and raped...

You have, Vallie.

Dubious consent, girl.

Shut the fuck up.

Too soon, the bathroom door swings open. I jump and grab my heart. I'll have a bruise there soon.

Donnie walks in, the mask in place, the dramatic downward curve now a creepy part of his identity.

Is he sad on the inside, too?

"Take off my brother's shirt."

I look at him in the reflection; seeing his masked form in the same vision makes it hard to separate the real emotions and the outer layers of protection I'm holding fast.

When I don't comply, his body encroaches on mine from behind. He glides his fingertips up the sides of my body and hitches the fabric as he trails them towards my ribs.

My heart moves into my ears. I raise my arms and allow him to remove the shirt. The view of too much flesh forces my eyes to squeeze the vision away.

Don't make me stare at myself naked while you stand behind me, gawking or silently mocking.

"Open your eyes," he presses his entire body to my back, the warmth confusing my senses.

I comply, blinking a few times before I return to my reflection again. *I hate him for doing this.*

"Look. Really look at yourself."

For the first time in a long time, I truly look at myself. Namely, my heavy, full breasts. They are a fucking problem. When I sleep on my side, they wedge between my biceps. When I stand, like this, they hang heavily and just... get in the way. They are the first thing to touch, well, *everything.*

My breasts are the main participants in every embrace, whether it's between a colleague or a family member I haven't seen in years. There they are, being pressed between me and their unwitting victims, when all I wanted was to offer a wholesome fucking greeting. *Ugh.*

"Beautiful," he says, and it catches me off guard because I was thinking the opposite.

I suppose they *are* symmetrical at least, heavier at the bottom, with peaks of brown I inherited from my Italian side.

I wonder when I became so self-conscious. Did it happen slowly or just appear one day?

"Touch them." His voice is deep and strained, but the mask adds detachment. At my lower back, his pelvis hardens, that's something he can't hide. "Massage them for me. I want to see you enjoy your big, beautiful tits."

I don't hate this.

But I should.

I lift my hands and start in a circular motion, lifting the weight and then lowering them again with each rotation. They are firm along the lower crease, heavy, and soft across the top and sides. I part my lips, feeling breathless all of a sudden.

Sexy, Vallie.

You feel sexy.

"Very good, Pup. Now press them together for me."

I press both sides together, creating a large, tight crease down the centre. My palms continue to knead each hard nipple, the pressure resonating between my thighs as though connected by a direct line of nerves.

Oliver rarely paid my breasts much attention. He said they only get in the way.

"You can decide how you want the next four days to go. You can sob and hold yourself at night. Or you can do as you're told. Trust that I won't harm you. Explore a new side of yourself. 'Cause all I want is my brother back. And you were begging for this on social media. Here I am... Are you going to behave? Embrace this? Then, I'll go. And you'll never see us again..."

I nod. "*Yes.*"

"Very good. In a red book, on page ninety, I found your annotation. Do you remember the scene? I won't give it away. Let's recreate it instead. It's odd that you read romance novels with curvaceous women when you're so unsure of your own sex appeal." His words are like chimes; they ring between my ears. "Face me. Drop to your knees on the tiles."

I don't hesitate or question why. Once again, I pretend it's because I'm acting the part, or maybe I've actually accepted what he has said. Or maybe...

You wish they actually liked you? Not just using you because you're Thirteen.

Ugh.

I swallow.

He places a big hand over both of mine and pushes them together, squishing my breasts into each other. "Like that. A tight pocket of pretty flesh. I'm going to fuck these lovely tits, and when I come, you'll catch it on your tongue, like a good pup."

I watch his tattooed hands, licks of ink wrapping around each digit, as he pulls his erection out through an open zipper.

I feel my eyes widen.

That's why it hurt.

He's lengthy and thick, with an angry vein that pulses when his cock jerks. The tip already leaks with arousal. *Is that what my body does to him?*

"You like it?" He nudges his cock at the crease. "Let me in," he says, his voice husky.

Letting some pressure go, I allow my breasts to go lax so he can push his cock in.

"Squeeze as tight as you can." He groans roughly. "I want to feel like my cock can't breathe."

His fingers wind through my hair as he starts to fuck my breasts, making me shuffle on my knees to keep steady.

Two eye holes stare at the spectacle.

I peer up at him, but he wrenches my head back, exposing my long neck. My taut throat hurts as I swallow.

"Head back. Mouth open." He wedges his leg between mine, kicking my thighs further out. He presses his shin to my pussy. I can't believe it, but I grind on him immediately.

"Let me see your tonsils," he pants.

My neck hurts as he tugs on the strands knotted around his fist. He lets loose, really, *really* pounding, and I hold them together to take his hard, brutal pace. I'm not sure he has any other speed. I swallow again and he snatches neck, halting me halfway, anchoring me to him with one hand in my hair and the other squeezing the air from me.

I need oxygen.

My lungs burn for it.

He presses on my throat until my tongue pushes out on its own accord and I pant, saliva rolling down the undulating muscle as it seeks air.

"That's a g-good fucking pup." His voice is wild and rough. "Pant and drool for a taste."

My eyes roll back as I move up and down his leg. Lose all my pride. Circle my clit on his jeans. Try to breathe. Lose all my sense of self. Unsure what the fuck has happened to me in the past few hours or how I'll ever be the same again.

I won't.

Do you care?

Yes.

His voice is all kinds of inhuman as he says, "Humping my leg like a good little puppy. Drooling for my thick, dripping bone. God, you're perfect."

His head drops back, a sound like a roar leaving his lips and filling the bathroom. Fingers claw restlessly in my hair. And his cock is enveloped in my breasts, the crown sliding up and out and then disappearing again. It is hot.

It's fucking hot.

"For the next four days, you're going to let me defile this body. Every inch will have been fucked red and raw. All your skin, covered in my sweat and cum. Bitten,"—he can barely finish his filthy promises— "Marked." A groan tears through his throat, and cum spurts across my chin and lips.

His hips pump hard.

I struggle to stay upright, but he guides me with utter control by his hold on my neck and hair.

"God, *yes*." He sways with his head back while I try to collect the fragments of my sanity.

When his head lifts again, he says, "Now, clean me up." He releases my throat. I inhale sharply.

Dropping my breasts, I let him drag me by my hair to his cock. I breathe in his scent—potent and masculine and not at all unpleasant. His hold tightens, and a warning crawls along my scalp, pulling a hiss from me. "Now!"

I lap my tongue out and clean the long length, hollowing my mouth to take him deep. Over and over again. I concentrate, a misguided need for praise spurring me on, wanting to show him how skilled I am. This is where I shine. Oliver always wanted blow jobs, never much else.

His hips churn, his flaccid monster cock growing within my suction and kneading.

"Fuck," he hisses, then tugs my hair and rips my mouth from him. Two eyes narrow through the eye holes, focused on my face. "You suck cock like you're starving. But I just fed you, Pup. No more until tomorrow. Now, bedtime."

CHAPTER 8

VALLIE

I hardly slept.

Donnie sat in the chair opposite my bed, watching me in his quiet contemplation as I tossed, turned, and ached until slumber grabbed me, and I leapt into its oblivion.

The next morning, he drives me into the city.

Did yesterday actually happen?

It's too surreal, yet as the sound of horns filter through the windows of Donnie's black SUV, this crazy reality hits hard.

The sun makes me squint.

I'm a hostage in broad daylight.

I was raped last night.

I don't know why I feel the need to repeat these things in my mind over and over. *I was raped. You were raped. I feel strange...* It's as though my body has already forgotten or am I in a kind of perpetual shock, or am I fooling myself, or, *fuck me,* am I actually... *okay? I shouldn't be.*

We park a street away from the courthouse.

Wearing a nice black dress with straightened hair and make-up, I appear as typical as any other day.

I squint through the passenger window as we pull over, a stream of suits and blouses passing by, followed by easy chatter. I want to scream at them, but I don't.

I'll play my part in this.

"Hey!" A girl raps her knuckles on the window, and I clutch my heart to stop it from beating through my ribcage. Fearful, I look over at her. No. I recognise her from yesterday, she's one of the other jurors.

The presence of Donnie at my side is like a knife scoring my skin, wanting attention. My eyes widen with a message for her; a silent warning *to run.*

She looks past me, her expression slipping to ungodly doom. She is staring at Donnie; his hoodie is tugged over the metallic mask, but the sad mouth and chin are still visible.

Her face washes to ice. A blue vein rises to the surface of her forehead and pulses with fear.

She knows him…

Without looking away, she steps backwards before staring at the ground and heading toward the court.

I look at Donnie, shocked and appalled. "It's not just me? How many other women are you fucking!" My voice pitches in a way that might suggest I'm jealous, so I pull on the seams of my composure. That's not what this is.

He grins, and I want to slap that smile off his face. "If I didn't know any better, Pup. I'd think you were being possessive." He laughs, actually laughs, in a throaty way. Stirring my insides with that sound, he manages to annoy and rouse me simultaneously.

Fighting with that truth, I growl. "Actually, I'm more worried about you giving me a damn disease!"

He laughs again. "I thought you were smart, Pup."

"What did you do to her?" For reasons that only bother me, I hate the idea of being one of many. It makes me feel dirty and insignificant.

"A friend of mine is watching over her grandmother. You two

are going to need to influence reasonable doubt amongst the other jurors, because I can't seem to track down their details yet." He leans in, and I get a whiff of cigarettes from his breath. "See, Louise likes to complain to strangers on the internet. Her entire life is on Facebook. It's rather boring, unlike yours."

"So, you haven't... You didn't?"

A slow grin touches his lips. "She's not my type. And you asked for this, remember? You asked to be kidnapped, to be fucked and used. I'm just the one who answered."

I swallow over a lump.

"Go in, Pup. Be a good girl. I'll see you here at four-thirty. If you try anything, if I get so much as a hint that you're being followed, I'll text my man, and he'll kill her grandmother. You understand? No one has to die. I'm only asking for a not-guilty sentence. Nothing more. Nod your pretty head and get out."

I nod and open the door, but he reaches out and grabs my elbow. The energy in the car shifts, his tone deepening as he rumbles, "Don't speak to *anyone* unless spoken to. Don't let anyone touch you. You see, while I'm touching you, you're mine. If I get a whiff of another man's scent on you, Pup, I'll bring out the screwdriver... Do you understand?"

It's just a threat, but it's a painfully visual one.

I agree with another curt nod. I'm pulling away from him when I feel his fingers protest, his hand reluctant to let go.

He finally does.

And I walk to the courthouse.

CHAPTER 9

TYLER

She puts her hand on my thigh. My body stiffens. My willy starts to get stronger, but I focus on the keys.

"Martha Argerich *was a showstopper by eight, but you're a dirty little boy who can't concentrate."*

I slide forward, trying to hide my willy beneath the keyboard so she can't see.

"You're too close. Back up."

Blood falls from my cheeks.

"Back up right now. You can't extend your arms if you hide your lap like that, silly boy."

I slide back along the stool, and her hand squeezes my upper thigh, her fingers brushing the inside.

Fuck.

My willy gets stronger and pushes up beneath my zipper, pulling a groan from me.

"As I thought," she purrs, her lips brush my ear as she says, "A dirty boy like you will never play like Argerich. *You don't want to finger those keys, do you? You want to stick your little fingers somewhere else?"*

I can't breathe.

I feel so strange.

My hair stands on end, and I can't help it. Something is taking over—something wrong. This is very, very wrong, and I don't want to feel it.

I don't want to like it.

I hit the keyboard harder, pronouncing each sound, bashing the melody to a crescendo of painful thundering.

She slips her hand into my lap, and for a terrifying moment, I think it might happen. Right. Now. So, I lock my teeth, the black and white keys blurring...

She grabs my willy.

Blood surges through me. My eyes bulge, tears suddenly drowning my vision, but I keep playing that angry tune.

Stop.

She starts to rub me there.

God. Stop.

An electric shock rushes from my balls to my willy, my forehead burns, and embarrassing pleasure shoots up and out.

A stutter of a whimper breaks from me.

My fingers fall from the keys, and I push her hand away as it spurts into my pants. I curl in on myself, hiding the wet stain as it grows, as I continue to fill my pants.

I sob into my lap as it leaks down the inside of my leg.

"Dirty boys don't play piano."

I wake with a guttural growl and lurch upright, my arms pulsing and swinging, beating the air as I fight the memories, defending myself from the phantom bitch.

Sharp breaths slide into my lungs like hot pokers, each intake agonising but necessary.

Feeling my talent, I lift my hands and watch them shake. The tattoos disguise etches in my skin, self-inflicted gashes made with a blade I used to hide in my bunk.

Under the slats.

No one looked there.

The pain of my genius was so fucking immense back then that I wanted to see my talent pour from me, from my skin, from my soul.

Crimson all over her black and white keys.

Damn, these meds!

They make my memories too clear.

I look around our girl's tiny house, more of a single-storey flat, and ache when the quiet circles me, mocking my lonely demons.

Not lonely for long.

She'll be home soon.

This one is different.

Special. She'll keep me, and I'll keep her.

I stand up, and my cock juts to attention, so I shove my hand down my jeans and grip it, squeeze until there is pain and start to jerk off as I wander around her home.

Our home.

I walk into her bedroom, seeing the covers bunched. I crawl on with one hand and bury my face in her pillow, inhaling her scent, her sweet tears, and her sweat. I squeeze and milk myself. I roll around on the mattress, like a fucking dog wanting to gather her scent and leave mine.

Humping my hand, I make a pocket between my throbbing cock and the mattress so I can smother my face in her sheets and jerk off at the same time.

A single key on the piano echoes between my ears, a continuous patter, flirting. It's nice. An A Minor.

Groaning, *I envision...*

Thirteen is riding me, her nipples skating along my mouth, sliding back and forth while I try to catch them, a pleasured smile on her lips—that *I* put there.

I pretend my fist is her—her pussy clinging to me.

Her body doesn't recoil from mine. She doesn't care about

my scars, not the criss-cross ones on my fingers where I bled my talent away. Not the ones on my cock, compliments of the wrong meds and an overwhelming desire to remove the dirty parts of me.

She doesn't mind them; she trails her tongue all over the smooth indents and kisses them gently. She doesn't cringe. She loves me the way I am.

Groaning into the pillow, I fuck my fist and pretend it's her on the other end of each hard stroke. I try to suffocate myself in her pillow, in her scent.

To focus on her.

Only her.

My free hand fists the sheets and I claw at them, pleasure building in my balls, drawing them into my body, and then—

Martha.

Fuck!

I roll to my back and stare at the ceiling.

Fuck. Fuck.

"Fuck!" I roar, picking up her pillow and throwing it towards a lamp, knocking the object to the ground.

CHAPTER 10

VALLIE

He kidnapped a six-year-old girl.

I can't even look at Donnie.

Meshing my body to the passenger door, I force angry space between us.

Out the window, I stare into the distance.

The sun drops behind a cityscape, creating a silvery band along the horizon.

My skin feels dirty, and my soul aches. It is day two of the trial, and it seems open and shut to me. Three witnesses were called, including the mother of six-year-old Molly Gray.

Fuck me.

There is no way we can get him a not-guilty verdict. Most of the other jurors practically walked away making noose gestures at Dexter.

Dexter.

He stood opposite the juror's stand, on the far side of the courtroom, in a suit and tie that made him appear like a football player at an awards ceremony—He looked hot.

He could get any woman.

Why would he want a child?

Features similar to Tyler, but weathered in the best way, with shorter hair and a close-cut beard, softly peppered with greys.

I tried not to look.

I tried so fucking hard, it was obvious. This monster kidnapped a little girl and did God knows what to her...

He deserves to be in jail.

Or castrated—or both.

Scowling out the window, I growl.

"Pup?" Donnie pulls into my driveway and cranks the handbrake. He pulls his hoodie back, the fabric bunching around his neck, a masked face staring directly at me. "I don't like this attitude. I hope you're not going to do anything fucking stupid. I know I've been playing nice—"

"Nice?" I blurt out.

Unbelievable.

He snatches my neck and squeezes until my eyes bulge. I clutch at his wrist, fighting the tight band.

He leans in. Cigarette-laced breath slithers across my lips as he hisses, "Very. Very. Fucking nice, *Pup.* I have been a goddamn Romeo in comparison to what I could do to you. I thought we were on the same page."

"He kidnapped"—The words breathe from a constricted throat— "a little girl."

"There has to be a reason."

"What could he possibly want with her?"

"My brother is not a paedophile!"

The passenger door flies open, the energy in the car freezing beside Tyler's presence.

Tension hovers thickly.

Idles on action.

"Our brother is not a paedophile," Donnie repeats, releasing my throat with a shove that pushes me into Tyler's awaiting hands. And it's crazy, but I cling to him.

Throwing my arms around this lunatic of a man, I bury my

face in his shirt, feeling connected, as though we are in this mess together. I'll demonise Donnie; it's easier.

This is a trauma bond, Vallie.

It's not real.

He is your captor, too.

He envelops me against his large, soothing torso. The cradling kind of movement to his embrace causes tears to rise behind my eyes. I hold those fuckers in.

Dipping his nose into my hair, Tyler murmurs, "Our brother is not a paedophile. Not after— Not because of… because of me. He wouldn't. He couldn't."

What is he saying?

Because of him?

Whatever it is, it causes my arms to tighten. He lifts me, cradling me against him as he walks into the house.

The sound of the car backing away and roaring down the street sends a shiver across my spine.

We close the door.

Locking us inside together.

CHAPTER 11

VALLIE

I'm so disgusted by what I heard today at the trial, that I rush straight to the shower. So horrified I let my feigned compliance slip in front of Donnie, I wash myself and focus on settling my trembling muscles and frantic pulse.

Do better.

Be smarter.

Stockholm syndrome: positive feelings for captors and sympathy for their beliefs. And, finally, negative feelings towards police and external figures.

I understand the assignment.

There is a camera on my bookcase, an old Polaroid. I need to get a picture of Tyler—of his face—while Donnie isn't here. Just in case I forget. I imagine a line-up, and all of a sudden, the faces blur, and... I've got to keep my cool.

I leave the shower, pull another dress on, and go to the kitchen, where Tyler's presence is potent.

And *watchful.*

I could get a knife, but what the hell would I do with it? And the grandmother who they have captive, what of her safety? I can't risk people dying. Compliance and waiting seem to be the right course.

Besides, Donnie always has a knife in his boot, so what does Tyler have? He's strong. Physically sleek, muscles unhidden even beneath his shirt.

Inhaling, I try to self-soothe. Listen to my pulse—I'm alive and resilient. Then it hits me how quiet the taps were... *are*. I turn the sink faucet on and stare into the stainless-steel trough, overcome by the silence.

He fixed the fucking tap.

I clear my throat—clear my thoughts. "Donnie fixed it?"

"He's good with a lot of stuff. Like I said, he takes care of us. Dex is always in and out of prison. I'm always in and out of..." he trails off. Coming up behind me, he stops close, his nose sliding into my hair. "Am I different today?"

He is.

"What are the meds for?"

"My talent," he whispers darkly, gripping my hips and spinning me to face him.

I meet his blue gaze, stunned by the heated intensity whirling within their depths.

He says, "I read one of your books while Don fixed your pipes. What do those words do for you?"

"They're not just words." I stare across the open-plan space, my gaze landing on my bookcase, lit-up with fairy lights, a wistful guiding light to fantastical loves and wild encounters. "They are about people who drop everything for each other," I muse almost to myself. "Who decide to act insane instead of appropriate." The words drag my gaze back to his gorgeous face, struck by the irony once again. "Who risk it all for *her*, whoever she is, and they don't conform or behave, and don't wait for love, they go and get it."

"So, they are like me?" He grins. "In the real world, girls don't always like that. I know I come on pretty strong, but I just decided one day that I wouldn't live at halfway. Not all girls like that..." He seems to disappear from his own gaze. "She called me a freak. Dirty. Wrong."

His jaw pulses.

"Who did, Tyler?"

"*Martha Argerich,*" he mutters, detached. The blue in his eyes seem to cloud as he loses focus. A memory stirs within him, and it's so close to the surface that, if I reach out, I could caress his pain with my fingertips.

I touch his forearm. "The famous pianist?"

He refocuses, finding himself quickly. "No. Not her." He leans past me and switches the tap off. I hadn't realised it was still running. "I get confused. My piano teacher."

"Were you in love with her?"

"Yeah."

I don't like this, but I don't push. *Positive feelings for captors...* "I don't like the word freak," I say. It's true, but it also serves my cause. "I've never thought of you as a freak, Tyler. You're a lunatic, sure. But not a freak."

His eyes roam my face, and it's catching—his passion, this spinning kind of adoration is *everything*.

"I'm going to fall in love with you," he declares. "Is that okay? You don't have to love me back. Just let me feel the way I want to at my own pace."

"See." I arch an eyebrow at him, and he frowns. "Lunatic. You can't fall in love with me so quickly. You don't even know me, Tyler—"

"But I do!" he insists. "I know that your eyes are brown but orange and gold when the light hits them. I know that you're an alto, but when you come for me, you're a mezzo-soprano, and when you came for Donnie, you were a soprano, but I don't mind that he got a higher register, because your orgasm with me lasted longer."

I swallow over a lump in my throat, my pulse a flutter in my neck. I place my hand over it, afraid he'll see the way his insane words make me feel. Make me hope. "Those aren't important things," I lie through my teeth.

"No? Your eyes are your soul, and your climax is your vulnerability. What is more important than those?"

Fuck. **Sympathy for their beliefs?** "You shouldn't make sense to me, Tyler." I try to smile.

"But I do." He looks at my bookcase that displays bookish merchandise: *Not Safe For Work* art, masculine scented candles, a bookmark that says *Spread Those Pages Like a Good Little Book Slut.* He sighs with a sweet grin. "'Cause you're a freak, too."

"Yeah." I can't lie. "I am. And perverted."

"Such a *pretty* pervert." He lifts his thumb, dragging it along his lower lip, watching me closely. "Do you get wet when you read those stories? I get hard when I play the piano."

Overcome by his proximity to me, by the heat and waves of volatile energy, by the fake syndrome that feels real, I answer him with a nod.

He bites that bottom lip with a hunger that is clearly meant for me, and I shuffle. "Can I watch?"

I blink at him. "What?"

"Can I watch you read one?"

"You want to watch me read?"

"Yeah." He grips the kitchen bench on either side of my waist, swaying his hips back and forth provocatively.

He squeezes the marble top.

I arch back but peer down at his forearms, seeing his sleeves bunched above his elbows, cords and veins pulsing under his effort to stay calm.

Fuck.

I love veiny forearms.

God, help me.

"I want to watch your body, baby," he admits in a deep timbre that throws his words directly to my pussy. "I want to see which parts make you shift in your beanbag, which make you lick your lips, gloss your eyes. I want to watch you get all tight and blush and—"

Gliding a tongue up the side of my neck, he groans as he collects my taste. "Then I want to lick you clean. Can I do that?" He leans back, catching me as I blush at the vision crafted by his words. "I don't want to force you, not like yesterday. I can see that was wrong. I got confused. I thought you loved me, but you don't know me. I thought she loved me, too. I was wrong. I'm wrong a lot."

Something like affection moves through my chest while my protective instincts want to wrap him in cotton wool. I'm a moth to his damn underdog flame.

Keeping eye contact, I peel one of his hands from the counter and thread his fingers with mine. When I swipe my thumb up and down his skin, I can feel those little grooves. Scars. They must be.

Another detail to note.

He has scars on his hands.

I walk him to my bookcase, letting his fingers slip through mine as I settle into my beanbag. I'll pretend that I'm alone, that this isn't completely fucked up.

A resting smile moves to my lips. I don't have to search for the right book. I know the exact scene I want to read while he watches me.

CHAPTER 12

TYLER

Relaxed on the sofa opposite her reading nook, with my back to the rest and legs comfortably wide, I watch as a telling blush crawls up her delicate neck. It settles into a pretty hue on her soft cheeks.

I swallow.

She flicks the page. Shuffles that luscious arse on the bag. The beans shift beneath her, sucking her in.

I'm gonna fuck her on that.

One day.

Maybe when she's pregnant.

And I *am* falling in love with her; my entire heart twists whenever she looks at me. And I hear a soft piano key sing with each bat of her long lashes.

This is it.

Everyone falls in love at first sight, but most are just too fucking fake to see it. Too rational. Too obedient to social formulas, norms, and conventions.

Love isn't a formula.

Love isn't sheet music. It isn't play and rest, go and stop. It's freestyle. It's letting loose on the keyboard until sweat drops and every cord of muscle in your arms throb from giving that piece everything.

You gotta love in freestyle.

She peers up from the butterflied novel, a hooded gaze meeting me through her lowered lashes.

Gazing down again, she directs my attention to her bare knees as they twitch with restraint. I like her legs. I like her little black dress, snug around her curves and ending at her upper thigh, showing the start of where they kiss.

"Spread your thighs," I demand.

She swallows, her eyes fluttering as she considers her next move. Her legs tremble. She parts her legs for me and traces the wet patch on her knickers, a slick line. She shows me her arousal. Up and down, she darkens the colour with more juices as she pleasures herself.

Blood roars through my veins, ballooning my cock until it's unbearably uncomfortable and viciously hot.

Hungry for her, I lick my lips.

I put my hand down the front of my jeans and grip my throbbing muscle. My heart beats in my palm, so I soothe it with long strokes, up and down, matching her pace.

Up and down, baby.

"Show me." I groan. "Push your knickers aside and show me your wet pussy. That's it. That's it." I stroke harder as she parts her folds, displaying her soft, pink insides.

"*Slowly*," I purr. "See, that's pretty. So pretty. Don't rush." She meets my every request. "*Mmm.* Put a finger inside now. Just one. *Fuck.* Yes. *See,* you're such a good girl for me. That's a piece of beauty."

She doesn't look up from the page, but I don't think she's able to read or concentrate because her eyes have a sheen of arousal and are glued in place.

"Dip further inside. To your knuckle. Oh. Fuck."

Precum leaks all over my hand, so I use it to lather my cock and work my shaft harder as it throbs to the beat of my rampant pulse.

I grunt, watching her, trying to keep my vision clear as pleasure seeks to fucking blind me.

"Push another finger inside. Show me how many you can get in. Yes. And another. Like that, baby. Show me how you'll stretch for me. For *us*."

Her head falls back on a moan.

She likes that... the *us* part.

"You want us both, baby? At the same time? How many of your tight holes can we use at once? All of them?"

Her hips lift off the beanbag, and I hear Widor; his precision of harmony, the emotive flow and ebb of sounds synchronising.

Beautiful.

So turned on, I beat myself off with an unrelenting fist, squeezing the tip and drawing down, fisting the root and choking upward as she reaches her *mezzo-soprano* register.

She's close.

"Such a good girl." I can barely breathe. "So hot and wet. Sweating for me. Panting. Pretty. Fucking yourself for me. Such a dirty little—"

"Whore," Donnie's voice severs the moment like a smashing symbol.

Martha.

Fuck!

CHAPTER 13

VALLIE

I have no idea what prevents my heart from tearing through my chest cavity as Donnie drags me from the living room under a potent wave of possessiveness.

"Get your hands off me!"

"Donnie!" Tyler barks, his voice close behind us.

Shoving me ahead, I can barely keep my footing until I'm inside my room, and Donnie is dragging my chest of drawers to barricade us in.

A fist beats on the door. "Dammit, Donnie! If you fucking hurt her!"

"You'll what, Ty? What the fuck will you do?"

Donnie shoves me backwards to the bed, as if to prove his point.

I bounce a few times before scooting away on my backside, my heart thumping to break free.

He switches off the light.

My vision fades to nothing.

Oh God.

Frantic, I search the space as my eyes adjust.

Upon me in seconds, Donnie has his knees on either side of my hips and both hands gripping my breasts.

He kneads the large mounds in a claiming way that feels wrong and domineering—my pussy clenches.

But… What the fuck? The scent of perfume and cigarettes stir together in the air, my nostrils burning from the aroma of his deceit and hypocrisy.

He's been with another woman!

While holding me hostage?

"You smell like perfume, you bastard!" I fight him, reaching up and swinging my palms around, hoping to connect with something. Anything. *Bastard!* "Get off me!"

"And you smell like wet pussy," he growls, grabbing both of my hands and banding them with one of his. He pins them to the mattress above my head.

The mask hides his face, but I can feel his breath. He feeds his free hand between us. Thick, demanding fingers slide under my dress and waste no time. Plunging into my pussy with ease, my incomplete climax still stirring, still leaking.

"Baby?" Tyler bashes on the door. "You okay?"

"So fucking wet," Donnie taunts, squeezing my wrists until I cry out in pain. "Leave your hands above your head."

"Or what?" I start, but he's already released me and is crawling down my body. I hear a rustling and a clink, the sound of him removing his mask.

The Polaroid… the camera.

Fuck… his head is up my dress.

I kick at him, but he begins to feast, and my efforts become meagre… *God.* That's- That's *good.*

This man doesn't just *eat* pussy. He fucks me with his tongue and bites my clit like a lion tearing into a carcass. My entire body shakes.

My eyes roll back.

I feed my fingers through his hair, exploring his features, but

I can't picture what I'm feeling while he eats me out. I have no spatial awareness at the best of times.

Pissed off with how my body responds to him, I take a fist full of his hair and dig my nails into his scalp. "Get your mouth off me!" I hold him to my pussy, even as I shred him. "You stink of another woman! This is so wrong. *Fuck.* S-so wrong."

Thrusting upwards, I nearly tear his hair out, but he fights back. He growls and sucks on me until I lose control of my limbs, my fingers pawing and fumbling with my melting mind. I'm so wound up from the intimate moment in the living room with Tyler—I want to come. I want to come so badly, even as I feel sick with jealousy.

"Shower the other woman off!"

"Possessive, little whore," Donnie snaps.

"Fuck you, Donnie!" Tyler growls through the door. "Don't talk to her like that!"

The barricade begins to scrape across the floor. The sound spurs Donnie to move, leaving me panting on the mattress with my dress bunched around my waist.

He switches the light on.

The sight of him in the mask makes me growl. *Keep your fucking face to yourself then.*

I tug my black dress over my head, exposing myself to him. I reach between my thighs and bear down on my clit. I need to get off. My thigh muscles hurt, burn, and perpetual spasms rush through me, never letting up.

I'm going to fucking explode.

The drawer continues to inch along the floor as Tyler fights to get into the room, but it's caught on my rug.

Donnie looks at the door, then lunges for me. He snatches my hand from between my legs, nails it to the mattress again, and leers at me.

"I'll make you come!"

Pain radiates through my wrist. "Then do it!"

"Do you like Tyler more than me, Pup? Is it the way he

fingers your wet cunt like he's playing the piano or the fact you have him fooled into believing you like him, too?"

"I don't like *you* at all!"

Liar.

Jealousy bulks his shoulders. "We'll see."

He rips his belt through the loops, the crack sounding in the room. Shoving his jeans down and ripping his shirt off, naked and perfectly chiselled, he stalks towards me.

Oh fuck.

Soon, he is grabbing my hips and flipping us over so I'm straddling him on the mattress. To prove a point—I want him. Well played, arsehole. I don't need to be pinned down. I want him so fucking badly, I'll ride him.

With a start, his fingers dimple my hips, and he forces me down the length of his monstrous cock. My pussy spreads wide, the muscles shuffling to accept him.

My body sets ablaze.

My core screams.

Weak with pleasure and pain, reeling from being impaled, I fall forward, my breasts mashing to his bare chest. *God*, he's hot and hard.

Sliding his hands behind me, he grips my arse cheeks and grinds me over him. As he does, he bucks, fucking upward, beating yelps of uncertainty from me.

The sounds are obscene and loud.

I can't even think.

Then he stops.

"What the fuck!" I protest.

Two eyes within the metallic holes shift over my shoulder. I swallow. I realise the sound of the drawer dragging against the floor has stopped.

Shocked, I twist on Donnie's lap to find Tyler a statue in the open door, staring at us.

His jaw muscles pulse, his teeth grind, and a soft humming sound comes from his throat.

"*Tyler,*" I exhale his name.

Beneath the dread of what this means, of what I've become, is desperate need. I want them both.

I manage to control my heart enough to speak to him. "Come here," I say softly.

Donnie lifts his hips, rolling me forward, working my clit on his pelvis in that effortless move. I moan but keep my body twisted so I can see Tyler.

God, I need to move.

Sweat slides between my breasts. I'm so fucking hot. Slowly, I circle my hips on Donnie but give Tyler all my attention. "Come here," I say again, desperation twisting my voice. I reach a hand back for him. "Please."

"Tyler." Donnie's tone is deep and commanding. "Come here. She wants you."

Stepping towards us, the beautiful lunatic doesn't remove his eyes from me as he unbuttons his jeans. Leaving them open at the top, the sight of lashes of scars trailing into neat, dark pubic hair causes my eyes to burn.

Is that why he doesn't remove his clothes?

The mattress dips as he comes up behind me, his thighs on either side of his brother's knees, his hot body a few inches from mine. I can feel his dark, jealous energy.

We all feel it.

And it's real.

Not one I'm faking.

Dammit.

I lean back towards him, seeking his lips, and he dips to me, wanting mine, our first kiss, so close, but Donnie bucks his hips, throwing me forward.

I cry out. "Arsehole."

Tyler soothes me. "It's okay, baby." Warm palms caress either side of my backside. "Hold still while I get inside you." Tyler's voice is deep and strained. He hums as his finger glides between my arse cheeks. The air around me stirs. "Have you had a cock in your little arse before?"

Donnie flexes inside me.

"Once," I moan and roll.

Tyler hums. Two fingers slide down, scissoring where Donnie fills me, collecting my juices. A wet trail moves upwards until he touches my flexing ring of muscles.

My eyes widen.

A chuckle leaves from behind Donnie's mask. "Get on all fours." His voice is dangerous. "Stick your arse in the air. Let my brother see your hole open and suck his cock deep."

The filthy words only make me moan.

Panting, I drop my elbows to bracket Donnie's head, bringing me close to him. His hands move up my sides. A blush hits my face. Up to my heavy breasts, he massages the outer swell and groans.

Dipping, he feeds himself one of my nipples, lathering it with his tongue. The mask causes friction and pinches, adding to my over-stimulated breasts. I whimper. He goes wild, filling the room with sucking sounds as he gorges on my flesh.

Tyler's cock meets my backside with a slap. The wet, hot crown slides up and down my thick crease.

Up and down.

My head spins.

Breath bated.

As Tyler lathers his length, I meet Donnie's intense gaze through his mask, so close that I can see him properly for the first time. His irises have flecks of light blue and green. The shared eye contact makes me want to know him, but the mask serves its purpose—detachment.

My hips rock on his cock.

Tyler presses through my rim.

"*Fuck*, fuck, fuck."

Fisting the sheets, I inhale steadily with each shallow thrust. Inch by inch, breath by breath, he defiles my tight hole.

He strokes the side of my plump cheek soothingly. "Your arse will look so pretty when you push my cum out, baby, and it slides between your creases."

I groan, synchronising the roll of my hips on Donnie's throbbing cock with the invasion behind me.

When Tyler's balls touch me, my arse full, I boil up from my ears to my temples, to my fucking marrow. He's too thick, so thick it burns, but the pain causes my pussy to weep all over Donnie.

"I'm so full," I whimper.

After a heavy moment of pause, the boys let me adjust, and my arse relaxes into the stretch.

Tyler's humming takes on a louder cadence, the rise in volume foreshadowing as he drags out, and I scream.

Then he's sliding in again.

"Fuck," he groans, pawing at my round backside.

"Squeeze us, Pup. I know you're desperate for what's inside," Donnie hisses, his cock stroking a bundle of nerves in my pussy as he joins his brother's push and pull of my body.

"*God.*" I fist the pillow.

Tyler stays deep, with short, meaningful thrusts, stirring my hips and breathing wildly. He has filled me in a way that curls my toes against the sheets.

"You're raw, baby," Tyler rasps. "You should see this, Don. Her arsehole is so fucking smooth. So pretty and pink. So tight and stretched around me. *Fuck. Yes.* Open for me."

God, I can't take it.

I shudder. "I'm going to come!"

Donnie pinches my nipple. "Come for us."

My climax coils, higher and higher, building through me, culminating in a throaty cry. My pussy locks on Donnie, and my arse puckers around Tyler. I squeeze every inch inside me, rippling around them in frantic pleasure.

"*Yes.* That's a g-good fucking girl." Donnie suddenly stiffens, his hands on my breasts kneading harder, the pace matching the pulse of his cock as he unloads inside my pussy.

"Fuck, fuck," Tyler groans, frustrated. "I can't. *Martha.* The fucking music. The fucking music!"

Donnie rears up, stabs his fist past my shoulder, and grasps his brother's throat.

"Come for our girl!" he growls, squeezing a groan from Tyler, demanding his orgasm in that violent act. "She's taking your cock, your cum, and she's fucking loving it. Come!"

Tyler's roaring climax releases in guttural growls as he drains his cock inside me, spurting hotly, pumping what seems like an indecent amount into my arse.

"Jesus, fuck," he bites out.

Fuck, that was hot.

His cock slides from my arse, and I collapse against Donnie's warm, hard chest. Our shared orgasms batter me into a loose, lethargic mass.

Exhausted, I forget that I'm angry at Donnie, forget who they are and all that has happened over the past few days. Fingers move into my hair, a tender exploration, and my heart inflates.

No, don't do that, Vallie.

Deflate it now!

Tyler pushes his cock back into his jeans and drops beside us on the mattress. He reaches over and pulls me from Donnie's chest, the soft fingers leaving my hair.

I wonder if I'm too heavy for him, but he's broad and packed with muscles, making me feel small and soft.

Am I no longer playing at Stockholm syndrome, or am I just an excellent actress? Seriously, I can see Oscars on the horizon.

Sighing, I exhale all that mess. I can't compartmentalise any of it. So I don't try to. It feels good. *They* feel *so* good. And I want to hate it. I want to cry, because I don't hate it!

Wrapping both biceps around my head, Tyler holds me to his thumping heart.

I close my eyes and listen to its frantic rhythm. Tyler couldn't come, even though he wanted to. Donnie had to help, like he understood, and I've read enough dark romance to suspect he's... been abused. *Martha? By his piano teacher? The scars, the humming, he's broken. God.*

I clutch at him.

A few moments pass.

The mattress shifts.

Donnie's large body slides away.

Batting my lashes in a sleepy, satiated haze, I watch Donnie's naked backside as he walks from the bedroom, each cheek a perfect cup, as if someone were holding them in place. It's impossible not to gawk—that man has junk in his trunk.

He's too stunning for words.

They both are.

With the two pieces I have, Tyler, who covers his body but exposes his face and heart, and Donnie, who masks the latter but walks around completely naked, I can puzzle them together into one complete entity.

I'm not sure I like the whole picture.

CHAPTER 14

VALLIE

Something pushes into my mouth, and even in my slumber, I suck it in deeper. But when a huge, smooth finger nudges at my arsehole, my eyes fly open to darkness.

Unable to see, I can only feel. My head is on Tyler's chest, his bicep lying across the top, holding me down under the weight of it.

His thumb explores my mouth.

A pool of drool leaves my lips, smearing his skin. I massage my mouth together around his thick digit as I come to. Blinking doesn't help my vision adjust, but the tips of my lashes brush something. I'm blindfolded.

Realigning with my body, I find myself in an odd position. My legs are spread wide; Tyler's ankles are hooked around the backs of my shins, holding my legs to the mattress.

I'm pinned to him.

"Stay still, Pup." Donnie's voice stirs fear and arousal through me, muddying all rational thought. The cool air licks at my pussy lips, cooling the moisture as it gathers.

A finger pushes into my arsehole. "I want to see my brother's cum leaking from you."

"Is it hot?" Tyler asks, rolling his thumb around my mouth, touching my gums, creating more saliva.

"So, so pretty and swollen from taking your cock." Donnie groans. "Is the puppy drooling?"

"All over me." Tyler chuckles. "Our girl is waking up."

A warm palm cups one of my cheeks, spreading and shaping the flesh. I can feel Tyler's cum dripping from inside me, leaking out as I pucker around Donnie's finger, a reflex I can't control, though I want to.

Immense heat blankets my face.

The gentle massage on my backside builds to groping and kneading, as though he's pumping my cheeks to push more cum from inside me. I clench again, wanting to stop the mess, but I only aid in what he wants. "That's a good girl."

Goosebumps race across my skin.

Involuntarily, I begin to rock against Tyler and press back into Donnie. But my eyes widen when something other than a finger pushes inside the tight ring of muscles.

"What's that?"

"Flex for me. Let me in." Donnie's voice deepens, lifting from his diaphragm like he's restraining himself. Something cold rushes inside me, spilling out again. *God.* "Cleaning my dirty puppy. She's so filthy."

His words spur a moan from deep inside me. Ashamed by how aroused I am, I suck on Tyler's thumb, using it to self-soothe, something to ground me.

Sweat mists my skin, adding to an overall sensation of being wet. Soaked. Every inch. Inside and out.

Then, lips touch my hole.

Two fingers slide into my pussy to distract me from the strange kiss, and I lock around them with desperate need, gripping in yearning as teeth suddenly bite the rim of muscles.

Tears stream down my face, drool leaves my mouth, and I ride his fingers while he tongues my hole.

"You like that, baby?" Tyler rolls his thumb again, massaging the gummy walls in my mouth, gathering moisture. I try to latch on to it. I'm grateful for his thumb. I gravitate to the motion, seeking comfort in it.

My entire body trembles as a sick sort of pleasure blooms from Donnie's devious kissing, biting, and licking.

"*That's it…*" Tyler soothes, his cock throbbing and wetting my stomach. "Let my brother lick your arse. Are you sucking his fingers in as eagerly as you're sucking on my thumb? Pulsing around his tongue?"

Wanton and crazed, I nod my head against his chest, riding the fingers inside me, guiding the penetration in and out at a steady pace that pairs with Donnie's mouth.

"*Please,*" I whimper; it has no meaning. I don't know what I want or why the word is dancing through my lips.

"I got you."

A ball of pleasure inside me grows and grows as he strokes along my clinging walls with long, skilled fingers while relentlessly nibbling the rim around my arse.

He bites down hard.

I shudder violently as my climax rears up from somewhere deep, ramming through me with force.

It's overwhelming.

This is wrong.

This is disturbing.

I want more.

The feeling arises from a dark place that likes the burn in my arsehole, the pinch of his teeth, the scooping of his fingers, the thumb in my mouth, the darkness, the depravity, the attention —*them.* And the way they both use my body while I can't see, while I can't move… I cling to the sensation as it pours through me.

I let it take me.

I let *them* take me.

CHAPTER 15

DONNIE

The small single-storey house on a derelict side of town is filled with the scent of herbs and flowers. The wallpapered walls are adorned with frames showcasing happy family shots—people just don't do that anymore.

"Third day of the trial?" Quinn asks, opening the front door for me and stepping aside. He's a short guy, disadvantaged in that way, but he's confident and loud-mouthed, so women like him.

I push my hoodie back, revealing my mask, and stroll in. I've become quite fond of my faceless existence.

"Yeah, a five-day trial apparently, but you never know. Could be four. Could be more. They are usually pretty accurate. Been to enough of Dex's fucking trials to know."

"The girl is playing ball?"

"The *girl...*" My mind swarms with images of my Curvy Thirteen riding my cock like her next breath would come from it. And the way my brother looked at her, *hell*, the way I was looking and feeling. *Shit.* I clear my throat. "Yeah. Dropped her off about fifteen minutes ago."

I don't want to talk about her.

"Was it as easy as you thought? The girl seems to be a bit of slut. Did you fuck compliance into—"

Heat hits my muscles. I slam him against the wall. "Shut your goddamn mouth!"

His small hazel eyes reflect the same shock I feel. "Okay, fuck. My bad."

"Donald? Is that you?" Kathleen's husky yet elegant voice comes from inside the house, snapping the tension.

Quinn smiles stiffly. "She's chatty."

Releasing him, I groan. I pinch the bridge of my nose and rub up into my eyes. I'm losing my fucking mind over a piece of pussy. This isn't me.

"*Jesus Christ,*" I mutter, shaking my head once with a small chuckle. "Does she know she's in a hostage situation?"

Quinn shrugs. "I mean, I told her. The old bat doesn't give a shit as long as we don't disturb her daytime TV and keep the prosecco and sliced pears coming."

"Kathleen. It's not Donald," I state, walking into the living room, finding her in a red leather recliner, eyes fixed on some crap on her old, tiny twelve-inch television set.

"Oh?" She twists in her chair, the leather creaking, her frail body slow and stiff to match. Squinting at me, she disagrees, "No. Your parents didn't name you Donnie. That's a girl's name. Your name is Donald."

For the love of— "Donatello," I correct, clasping my hands in front of me and staring at her through my mask, which was supposed to inflict terror but... I'm very rarely wrong—arrogant for a reason—but I've been floored over and over the past few days.

She doesn't look up. "What?"

"Donatello, Kathleen. My parents named me Donatello." I move to stand in front of her, and she squints up at me again, sceptical. "It's Italian." I don't know why I explain, but I add,

"My mother is, *was*, Italian. My brothers got Anglo names, I got the Italian one."

"Oh…" She looks me up and down as if to judge for herself. She nods. "Well, I can't see you properly anyway. So, I was watching that Jerry Springer—"

"Fuck," I laugh, but I've no idea where that cheery fucking sound came from. "What year is it?"

"2023, dear," she answers seriously. "Are you alright?"

"Yes, I just meant that's an old show, so…" I pause, rolling my eyes at myself for indulging this for so long. "Just… Fuck. Nevermind."

"Oh, okay, dear. So, the young woman cheated on her partner." Kathleen takes a sip from her prosecco and slips a pear slice in her mouth, enjoying both flavours at once.

She nods slowly, visually judging the taste.

"Hmm. Bit tart." Then she swallows and says, "She gave another man, I think she called it, a blow job."

"*Jesus Christ*," I spit out.

"And I thought, *poor* Stephen."

I can't believe my ears. "What?"

"Stephen," she repeats as if I should know who that fucker is. "My husband."

"Right."

She goes on, "*Poor* Stephen lived his entire life, bless his soul and cotton socks, without ever experiencing a blow jo—"

"Oh my fucking God, Kathleen."

"I'm sure you've had one."

Cutting the conversation there, I wander over to her and snap a picture to send her granddaughter. "Well, I'm glad to see you're well. Do you need anything for the time being? It'll only be a few more days."

"Oh, okay, dear."

On my way out, I stop and say over my shoulder, "You know, you nearly got me in trouble with a girl yesterday. You want to tone down the damn perfume in this place or what?"

"Oh, I'm sure you get yourself in trouble just fine without me, Donald."

Well, fuck me sideways.

CHAPTER 16

VALLIE

Sitting through another day of this trial is tortuous, and I can't concentrate which isn't bad as all signs point to a guilty verdict.

The evidence that he took her, that he was with her at a hotel, where she was found… are all irrefutable.

So, I let my mind drift. Emotions swirl through me as I replay the past few days in my mind.

Donnie forced himself on me.

Tyler licked and fingered me to the longest, most beautiful climax of my life, all while I was in shock.

Then we did something… all three of us. And it wasn't dubious in nature. It was outright lustful consent—screaming consent—*yes*.

I understand why I should have kept repeating what happened to me in my mind—I was raped. I was raped, I was raped. Because raped has morphed into *forced*. Into *yes*.

And Donnie and Tyler…

They aren't unwelcome anymore.

Perverted lunatics, hell yes.

But not unwelcome…

By the time I've thoroughly diagnosed myself with psychosis, PTSD, and *real* Stockholm syndrome, the jury is being dismissed for the day, and I'm taking the steps outside the courthouse to the city street below.

"Who is he?" I hear a roar of anger and see Oliver charging towards me, his fists pumping on either side of his hips, his face screwed together in fury. "I saw him, whore! At your house!"

It happens fast.

I'm shuffling backwards when he's upon me, the back of his hand swinging and connecting with my cheek.

The crack of sound bleeds my ears.

Pain flashes through my skin, throwing my face to the side and blackening my vision.

His slap disorientates me.

I freeze up for a second. Just a second. And he's grabbing my upper arms, shaking me, rattling the world, the street, the onlookers, back and forth.

"We broke up!" I screech, trying to fend him off as random voices soar around me.

"Hey, man! Go easy."

"I'll call the police."

"Let her go!"

Their words are there, clear and strong, but no one intervenes. Oliver is big; he's a burly, heavy arsehole, fuelled with a scary intensity. One closed-fist punch from his weighty arm could render a man unconscious or worse.

"You filthy, fat slut." His words hit my soul. "Everyone told me I was too good for you."

"Believe them and fuck off!" I raise a shaky hand and tear my nails down the side of his jaw, panting and growling until I draw blood. "Let me go!"

Everything races; moments rush by like a flashing montage of images.

Oliver is suddenly hauled backwards by the collar. A black gloved hand fists the fabric. A ghost-like figure marches him to the fountain, throws his face into the watery depths, and plunges him beneath the surface.

The world slows to an eerie breeze.

I walk forward, and the figure looks over its shoulder, shocking me with gorgeous features, chiselled and angelic, conflicting with a distant, cold, blue gaze that screams of death, pain, and possessiveness.

"Tyler," I breathe. *No. No.*

Too overwhelmed by his intent to hurt, he faces forward again, using his strength and singular focus to hold Oliver's gasping mouth beneath the water as he thrashes.

Bubbles collect around his head.

Vomit stirs in the fountain.

If he vomited, then…

He's asphyxiating.

God, Tyler's going to kill him.

I shoot around in a circle, the press of people, of alert eyes, of witnesses, pulse frantic protectiveness through me. Citizens watch—recording.

God, no.

Get him out of here, Vallie!

And the final component hits hard: **Negative feelings towards police and external figures.**

Lunging forward, I tug on Tyler's pulsing bicep, enough to disturb his focus, allowing Oliver's mouth to breach the surface. The gurgling sound churns my stomach.

Tyler throws his arm backwards, shoving me away. I fall to the pavement and gape at the spectacle.

I just fucking watch.

As Oliver stops thrashing.

As Tyler doesn't give up.

I'm not sure when it ends, whether it's seconds or minutes, or anytime at all, but Tyler is approaching me, and I'm in his arms in an instant.

In disbelief, I stare over his shoulder as I'm carried from the scene. A body lay in the fountain, the head disappearing into a cool, watery grave.

A car revs angrily.

Then we are in it.

Tyler slides me across the backseat, belts me in, and Donnie pulls into oncoming traffic.

Car horns blast my eardrums. I grasp at my chest, holding the frantic organ inside.

You killed someone, Tyler.

Donnie's angry barking echoes. "God dammit, Tyler! Fuck. Fuck. Fuck!" He throws the car up the curb, cutting the sun out as he tunnels between two large buildings.

People jump out of the way.

Oh, God, I just saw a man die.

Tyler is silent and still, but when I look at him, his throat vibrates as he hums something that can't be heard over all the other aggressive sounds.

We appear on the other side of the buildings, dropping into a one-way lane.

The car slows down.

I try to breathe.

I just saw Oliver die.

Setting a normal pace, Donnie filters cautiously through traffic before changing direction and circling around. I'm confused, blinking out the window as everyday life passes, but then we are on the highway and heading towards home.

My home.

CHAPTER 17

TYLER

I couldn't let him live.

I walk into her house, rocking myself to the melody of Widor and the memory of my girl's pretty orgasm from last night. I had to do it. I had to stop him. He hurt her.

"I did what I had to do," I ground as Donnie closes the front door behind us. He locks it and rounds on me.

"You wait!" He grabs a fist full of my shirt and our girl watches on in shocked horror.

I wish that she hadn't seen that. That's my only regret. Having to push her away so I could do the deed, having her know and see.

Yeah, that's my only regret.

I smile, proud. "I did it for us."

His fist tightens on my shirt, twisting the fabric. *Don't be mad, brother.* "You skipped your antipsychotic this morning, didn't you?"

"Just the one." I shrug.

"That's the fucking fast release! You need that one until the others kick in! Damnit, Tyler!"

"I felt good this morning."

"We could have sorted the douchebag out another time! In private!" He releases me and snaps around, lifts a chair, and throws it against the wall, the wood splintering into pieces. "Not in front of the entire damn city!"

Vallie gasps.

Baby, it's okay.

I walk to her, cup her cheeks, and stare into her brown-sometimes-orange-and-gold gaze. "I'd do it again, baby. He touched you."

She pants, bringing her hands up to cover mine. Our eyes meet, our connection sails around us to a C-Major-9 chord. Such a beautiful, longing sound that adds elegance and length—a forever—to any piece.

Her fingers swipe the surface of my skin, over the grooves and cuts, a question flashing in her gaze, yet it's gone just as quickly as it appeared.

But I understood it: *what are these?*

"I cut my talent out, baby," I answer her because I'll tell her anything at this point.

"*Jesus Christ,*" Donnie curses, storming into the bedroom and slamming the door shut. Damage control. That's what he's all about. "He'll take care of this."

"No," she disagrees, but she doesn't understand; Donnie fixes everything. "They have your picture, Tyler. And mine, and Oliver is…" Her lower lip wobbles, so I go for it.

I kiss her.

I hold her face and mash our mouths together, feeling her lips wobble between mine until they join my gentle rhythm. She kisses me back. She. Is. Kissing. Me. Back. And the whole fucking world sets to a wild spin.

Pouring all my feelings into this kiss, I offer her meaning and answers with each stroke of my tongue.

I understand you're sad, baby.

I know it's scary to see.

But I did it for you.

I love you.

We're okay.

I did it for you.

Her perfectly pitched moan elevates to a mezzo-soprano whimper, and I'll remember the music she made when we first kissed for the rest of my life.

I deepen the kiss, feeding my hands back through her hair. She matches me, lip tug for lip tug, lick for lick. My heart tics to explode in my chest.

"Why?" She cries into our kiss, her voice vibrating against my lips. "Why did you have to do this? It could've been okay." Tears fall into our mouths. "I could have accepted you. And Donnie. And forgiven you. For all of this but now…"

What? I pull from our kiss, her words twisting.

"But now what?"

If the look in her eyes could beat my body to a bloody pulp with reality, it just did. Pools of disappointment and pain stare back at me.

What do they mean?

What do they mean, baby?

Am I an idiot? Was I wrong?

Like with Martha?

Was that —

Was that not what she wanted?

Like in her books?

Touch her and die?

"Didn't you want me to do that, baby?"

Startled by my words, her eyes become discs, wide and full of fear or contempt or—I don't know, *dammit*, I can't read her.

She lowers her voice. "You think I want you to kill someone for me? To kill my boyfriend?"

Boyfriend… No. No.

I'm stepping backwards, shaking my head, as the space around me suddenly feels too small, pressing in on me.

'Dirty boys don't play piano.'

"Shut up!" I bark at her words.

Martha's version of Mozart's Piano Concerto No. 20 in D minor suddenly rams into my ears, drowning my thoughts. *No.* My cock gets painfully hard, leaking and throbbing with a frantic and angry heartbeat.

No. No. No. Fuck.

'Are you in love with me, dirty boy?'

"Don't do that," our girl whispers, reaching me inside my memories. Her terror-filled eyes lock on my hands.

I follow her gaze. I realise I'm in the kitchen holding a knife to my knuckles, pressing the blade in deep, feeling the slow trickle of blood as it leaves my pulsing veins.

My cock pounds with heat and hate; my zipper stretches as it tests it strength.

I'm staring at the blade, pretty and metallic, the crimson making a smooth line that shines and sparkles, when she touches my hand—the one holding the knife.

I don't know when she stepped into the kitchen, but she's coaxing it from me.

"Give it to me," she insists softly, taking the blade from my hand and placing it on the countertop. Should I be concerned she has access to a knife? *Is this still— Am I still meant to keep an eye on her?*

"You don't have to do this," she says, her sweet voice carving into my thoughts.

I look into her eyes. "I cut the talent out of my fingers. They don't fucking play anymore."

Breathing hard, she collects a kit from under the sink and begins to bandage my knuckles, the tender touch like nothing I have ever felt before. Caring. Careful. "We broke up, Tyler." She reads me so well. "He is my *ex*-boyfriend."

"You're lying, baby."

"Vallie. I'm Vallie. And I'm not." She doesn't look at me as she works on my hand, but I stare straight at her. Each inch. The curve of her nose, the bow of her upper lip, the dimple in her left cheek. The entire stunning canvas of *Vallie.* "Your talent wasn't dirty. It's special. Whatever happened—"

"I fell in love with her."

"How old were you when you fell in love with her?" With her head down, her voice is cautious and gentle to match.

"Ten. I think."

"And she touched you?" I see the roll of her throat as she asks this question. She doesn't look at me, but her inquiry is intense enough without eye contact.

"I think so."

"You think so."

"I thought she did. For a long time. I thought she kissed my ear. Touched my thigh. Held my cock while I played, and then when I came…" My cock throbs again. "She took it all away. Called me dirty."

"You're not dirty."

"My talent is."

"*No*," she says, but she doesn't understand. She hasn't seen. She can't understand. She wasn't there.

My body tenses, my cock drips, and I growl. I pull my hand from her, grit my teeth hard, and rip open my top button.

I reach in and fist my cock, squeezing it and moaning long and hard. *Fuck.*

"Look," I snarl, stroking up and down. Up and down. I squeeze some pressure out before displaying my full length on my palm for her to see. The entire thick shaft is slashed in grid-like scars from years of trying to bleed my dirty talent out. "*See.* I should have cut it off, but I couldn't. Should have, but—"

Shaking, I brace for her repulsion. A vein in my cock thrums, the scars shift around the beating channel, and I wait.

"I know what it's like to be embarrassed by your body, but..." Tears fill her eyes. "But this is..."

"Don't lie to me. No one wants this. No one wants to touch my cock. No one—"

Then she drops to her knees, cutting my words off at my tongue and my thoughts out completely.

She takes my cock into her smooth, little hand, the thick throbbing muscle looking huge and mean in comparison.

She kisses the tip.

My breath hitches.

Tilting her head, she laps her tongue along my heavy, pulsing length. Touching all the scars, rolling over the ridges and valleys they etched into my skin, she kisses me again.

I freeze.

Then she takes my cock into the hot, warm depths of her mouth with a skill that sends shockwaves of energy through my spine and a perfect melody into my ears.

Her glassy eyes find mine, and I touch her soft cheek with my thumb, swiping over the blush.

I love you.

She starts to work my shaft like a damn icy-pole, hollowing her mouth to take me deep before sucking and drawing out until she reaches the tip. Then, swallowing the entire thing again. And again. And again.

"*Oh, fuck,*" I bite out, breathless.

Dark dots dance in my vision.

My thighs tense to the point of pain.

My balls draw up, my hips start to rock, and she meets my thrusts. Her hands support herself on my thighs as she cradles my cock in her mouth, the tip touching her throat.

"*Fuck.* Your mouth. So good. You like my cock, baby? You like it dripping on your tongue?"

Suddenly, in my mind, a cascade of precisely paced and flawlessly placed keys build—a crescendo of euphoric sounds. I lose focus, and dark bliss hazes my vision. Her mouth is hot, wet, warm—everything I ever dreamed of.

She doesn't care about the scars, Tyler.

Thrust.

She is kissing them.

Thrust.

She's licking them.

I'll kill everyone for her, I don't care, I'll do anything to have her like this, for this woman, I'll bleed and burn and fight!

My head drops backward as I fuck her mouth. Enjoying the warmth, the love, the understanding, no shame, *God, yes.*

"*Vallie,*" I hiss, losing strength to shudders, losing my mind to her and the powerful and resonant notes in my mind.

Vallie. Vallie. Vallie. Yes.

"I'm gonna come, baby." I tense up. "What do— Do you want me in your mouth? On your face?"

She sucks me in deep, and I explode as the final chord of my climax pounds through my ears.

I come. I come so fucking hard that every inch of muscle inside me shakes. I fill her throat, but she swallows around my crown, milking the final spurts from me with each contraction.

My cock slowly slips from her mouth. Tremors rocket through my body as it falls through her wet, warm, loving lips.

She licks a bead of cum from the corner of her mouth, and her eyes soften as she says, "Was that your first blow job?"

I nod, still reeling. "I don't let anyone see."

"You're gorgeous, Tyler." She reaches up, her body rising as she lifts to her tippy-toes. Her hands cradle my cheeks again. "I'm not kidding. You're the single most stunning man I have seen, and girls would scratch at each other to drop to their knees for you."

My teeth crush together, my molars aching against the pressure. "I don't believe you."

"Oliver used to call me his '*chubby girlfriend,*' and I started to identify like that. He'd slap my arse but not in a sexy way, in a way that made me feel like he wanted to mock the way it wobbles. He would tell me when something was too tight or..." Sadness moves through her gaze, and I want to kill him all over again. "Don't believe her. The voice in your head. She's a liar."

"The scars?"

"I'm fucked in the head, so don't take this wrong, but..." A blush moves across her cheeks. "I think scars are sexy."

CHAPTER 18

VALLIE

I'm wary of leaving Tyler alone, so I give him one of my favourite spicy books and tell him to read it. I sit with him on the sofa and stare. When he's like this, he's boyish and unsure but still sexual, living inside a very adult male body.

So this is me now...

This is what three days with the most beautiful and damaged individuals have done to me. I'm aching for a broken man who sexually assaulted me while yearning and keening for his brother who raped and demoralised me.

I'm living a dark romance.

I try to swallow it all down, like a very tangible entity, push it away, to the depths of me, out of sight, out of mind, so that I can think rationally again... *Nope.* It doesn't work. My fucked-up feelings for them are cellular.

I go to leave but Tyler reaches for me. "No. Stay! You're mine. I want you."

He looks about ready to throw me down if I say no, so I grip his hand, using my thumb to brush the scars, to caress and love them. He looks at my thumb.

"I'll come back." I smile. "I'm going to let myself fall in love with you, Tyler. I'm going to start falling right now. Is that okay?"

His brows tighten, distrustful. "You don't know me."

"Yes. I do." I shuffle closer. "I know that your eyes are blue when you're resting, but when you're lost in thought, they appear almost grey, like they are clouded with the same confusion that's in your mind. I know that when you come, you growl from your throat, releasing all that pain and letting go."

He inhales sharply, repeating my words back to me. "Those aren't important things."

"No? I know your soul. *And* your vulnerability. What is more important than those?"

I lean in and kiss him.

After a few minutes, I can't waste any more time, needing to act. I stand and leave him on the beanbag with the book on his lap and my affection dancing in his eyes.

Hesitation fills my stomach with air as I stand outside my bedroom, and, to my fucking shock, I almost knock. I almost knock on my *own* fucking door.

Go in there!

Walking in, I find Donnie sitting on the corner sofa, staring at my bed with his phone in his fist, the display still bright from recent activity. A smoking cigarette is pinched between the fingers of his other hand, the bright cherry dying at the filter.

"I don't like you smoking inside." It's the dumbest thing I've ever said, but it's a statement that holds weight—I'm no longer his to control. I want some authority back.

"He isn't dead. They revived him."

His words press a deep, relieved exhale from me. "Thank God. That means—"

"Do you like my brother?" He stares as the ember flares and slowly melts to dust. "Or is it an act?"

Did he just ask me that?

Like he hasn't been threatening to stab a screwdriver into my eye?

Like I'm the one who owes them something. Fuck him.

I grit my teeth and answer him honestly. "I do—"

"Don't fucking play with me, Pup!" He rises to his full height —a height that looms.

My fingers twitch to throw something at him, but the stiffness in his posture, the stillness to his breath, hint at genuine concern. And I'm a moth again... this time to his damn show of vulnerability. "The truth, Pup."

"I do." I cross my arms over my breasts. "I like *him.*"

"Good." He walks straight at me. "I need you to protect him."

I shuffle backwards until the wall hits my spine, pushing air through my lips. "Why?" I breathe. "What's going to happen now?"

"The police will be here soon." He stops close to me; I can see his lips in the hollow of the sad metallic curve. "Oliver would have told them what happened. It's all been recorded. I just watched it streaming on the news. They will come for Tyler. They'll lock him away in a ward again."

I cover my gasp, shaking my head and talking. "Oh God. No. I can talk to Oliver or..." My eyes drop to the carpet, my mind stirring with images and consequences.

Will they know I'm on the case? That I wasn't honest? That I was hiding my connection to them... Or wasn't hiding it, but I was extorted? Threatened.

"Look at me," he says, and I snap my gaze back to him. "When they get here. You need to tell them that it was *me.* That I attacked the arsehole."

"But— but—" It's not possible. "They have footage."

The eerie mask stares at me like it wants to dive into my mind and check my intentions.

Can he trust me?

It takes all my tolerance not to growl at him for that sceptical look. *Damn him. He is the one who did this to me, but he doesn't trust me?*

The pause is heavy, then he lifts his hand, reaches back, and with a big exhale, he slowly removes his mask.

Hairs rise on the back of my neck.

My eyes widen on the most stunning and familiar face. Cheeks like the plane of a chiselled diamond. Eyes, blue and bright. "Identical," I breathe.

"Identical twins," he confirms.

Now, seeing his mouth move, his voice soar through his lips, the pulse of his cheeks, the tight weave of his brows, *yes*— that's Donnie. I can imagine him now, beneath me last night, inside me, when our eyes lingered in hate and something else.

"They'll know you're on my brother's trial," he says, schooling his expression. "So, you need to tell them I've been holding you hostage, threatening you, and I need you to tell them that I tried to kill Oliver because he knew too much. You have to do this. They'll take you off the trial because you can't be objective anymore."

"But your brother's case?"

"I still have Louise's grandmother."

My stomach knots up.

My eyes roll over his face. The real Donnie is a thing of enchantment, and my gaze is mesmerised by the way his mouth wraps around words of authority, by his serious expression. I reach up, rising to my tippy-toes, and touch his smooth cheek.

His brows furrow.

"What will *you* do?" I ask.

He pulls my hand from his face. I try not to flinch from the rejection. "I'll take off."

"Now?"

"Right now."

"How will you fix this?"

He places a palm on either side of my head, caging me between him and the wall. "I'll sort something out, Pup. I always do. But *you*..." He lowers his face, his mouth stopping inches from mine, his breath racing down my chest. I grip the wall behind me, my fingers flexing on it. "Need to protect Ty for me. He's fragile. He's vulnerable. I won't have him go back to the psych ward. He dies in there."

My heart is twisting.

I don't understand it...

He lowers his nose into my hair, lingering, so close to rolling his cheek against mine, but... not. It feels like goodbye, and hello. It feels wrong. My throat thickens.

Don't go.

"And he'll protect you, too, Pup." He chuckles softly. "From other men. From your loneliness."

"I only need protecting from you, and you're going away." My voice is strange. Angry. In pain. I don't know. The words gnaw at something inside me. To compensate for the tone and the emotions riding it, I agree. "I will protect him."

"Well," he laughs sadly. "Seems you're not the girl I thought you were. You're a hell of a lot more."

He pushes off from the wall, and I inhale deeply, sucking in the air his presence was effortlessly squeezing from me.

He walks to the bedroom door. "You haven't posted in a few days, Pup." He looks over his shoulder. "What will your followers think?"

I can't move from the wall, feeling stuck, glued with emotion. My legs threaten to give way if I try.

Biting my bottom lip to stop it from wobbling, I shrug sadly. "Maybe they'll think that I've been kidnapped."

"Aint life funny."

Then he leaves the room.

Continue their story and meet the infamous Dexter Vaughn in Curvy Forever – part two in the Curvy Thirteen Playlist.

BOOK TWO: CURVY FOREVER

Continue the story with Vallie, Tyler, & Donnie, and meet the notorious Dexter Vaughn...

I wonder what he'll bring to the table... or should I say shower...

Wanna join my Newsletter for new release updates?

You: I'm not sure I like email marketing...

Follow me on Bookbub for new release alerts?

You: Yeah... I also like Facebook...

Join my reader group?

You: Okay, okay. I'll do all three. You seem really nice and I bet you're also cool and generous and kind... Just saying.

Thanks, imaginary reader. Did you know that there is a teaser scene on the next page?

You: Whaaaaaaat?

CURVY FOREVER
TEASER SCENE

A knock forces my eyes to the back of my head.

Fan-fucking-tastic.

I know it's not Oliver, because he's still mumbling incoherently in the hospital. As soon as I can, I'm getting a restraining order.

But the police have been at my front door three times in the past four days, so it's safe to assume it's them. A routine check, they say. But I think they suspect me.

They are all too eager to peer past me and into the hallway, looking for Donnie, or lies, or clues.

For now, they have no evidence to arrest me or to attain a warrant to search the house, so I've been playing my part and acting the nervous victim, but it's wearing on me. I've never been very good at playing victim even when I was... even when I was Donnie's victim.

Glancing over my shoulder, I check that my bedroom door is still closed—Tyler's asleep in my bed.

I walk to the front door, plastering on my figurative victim-face, ready to go round four with the crew in blue. I rub my cheeks and swing open the door, finding a postman with a...

What the actual fuck?

"Morning, Miss," he says, brightly. "We have a delivery for a Valentina Relli. Is that you?"

Words allude me as I stare at the item set down on the porch; a silvery dog cage large enough for a Rottweiler or a Doberman —*or a human.* There is a bow on it.

Of course there is.

I blink, and the man clears his throat. "Miss?"

"Yes." I nod, swallowing over the lump of passion wedged in my throat. "That's mine, I mean, that's my name."

Signing for the cage, I try not to smile but my traitorous lips want to embrace this message.

The man leaves me on the porch.

Circling the cage, I clutch my hips and study the lavish enclosure. The bow is pink and large, carefully tied to the top and displayed like a flower, the ribbony tale long enough to cover the entire roof.

I reach out and touch the silk. Then I see a small note tucked beneath the fabric. Warmth and discomfort stir through me, filling my chest. I pull the note away from the metal roof and open it to typed words.

Still tucking you in, Pup.
Get comfortable.
D

I beam.

Bastard.

Couldn't he just send fucking flowers?

Like a normal person. But then, we're not a normal couple... Are we a couple? Not a normal... collective... *Ugh.* We're not normal!

I don't know how to feel. Maybe I'm meant to feel a sense of dread, a shiver of threat, a deeply unsettling weight, but my heart is warm and airy.

My hands shake.

The cage is an answer to my *what-ifs*…

To the ones that have been festering in me since Donnie left. What-if the connection I felt wasn't real, a manifestation of my need to please and be liked. What-if he uses me to protect Tyler, until he doesn't need me anymore, casting me aside? What-if I don't embrace this thing, this pull between the three of us? What-if I fuck it up?

God, I don't want to wake up one day, alone, old, bored out of my mind, and realise the Vaughn brothers are my regretful *what-if*…

The cage tries to answer that.

Yeah, it's a talkative cage.

Now to get it inside. I'm fumbling with where to grab it and how to lift it when I hear, "He's never been subtle."

The mysterious voice strokes me, from the tips of my ears to the points of my toes with its smooth, rich quality; a lasting deep timbre that mists my skin in sweat.

Slowly, I straighten and turn to face the man with the commanding tone, anticipating another officer. This will be hard to explain to them; I'll have to get a dog. And I don't want a dog right now.

"Can I help—" My words become heavy on my tongue when I see Dexter Vaughn strolling up the driveway in a suit that seamlessly moves with his form, displaying his agile gait and showcasing the muscles in his thighs, the reach of his broad shoulders, the—

Stop staring, Vallie!

I clear my throat. "What are you doing here?"

"Bail. Thanks to a retrial due to a compromised juror."

He halts at the bottom of the steps and clasps his hands in front of him, resting them against the lush material of his suit. He has money. I never thought to ask…

Do the boys come from money?

He gestures to the cage, his expression effortlessly charming, a smooth, well-defined angular face that resembles a goddamn work of art; freshly shaven, contoured cheeks; his brother's blue eyes.

"Where is my little brother? Surely, he could have assisted with this..." He muses on the cage. "Item."

"He's asleep," I mutter, then curse at myself.

Fuck, Vallie.

Can you trust this guy?

I tell my hormones to chill the fuck out. *He kidnapped a little girl... He's a monster.*

My cheeks don't listen, blooming a rosy hue to match the rising heat inside me. "This is for my dog. I have a dog. A big one. He's huge and mean, actually."

Dumb.

He grins, and *God.* "You don't have a dog. Would you like me to help you with that? You need only ask... *sweetly.*"

Is he serious? I scoff. "I can do it myself."

"That lie won't benefit you. Tell the truth."

Holy fuck, me.

His irresistible magnetism forces the truth through my lips. I admit through a small voice, "I can't lift it."

"Well." He takes the three steps up to me, forcing me to lift my chin and squint as the sun cuts around his body. Then he casts a shadow over the porch. I'm floored. Can't think or breathe or function. He wraps his fingers around the top handle and lifts it. "It's a good thing I'm here. Isn't it, baby girl?"

Continue reading...

THE BUTCHER BROTHERS

Have you read Max and Cassidy's epic love story?

Blurb:

The city's golden girl falls heart-first into a dark underworld.

I want two things in life: to be the leading ballerina in my academy—
And Max Butcher…

A massive, tattooed boxer, and renowned thug. And my very first
crush…

I may be a silly little girl to him, but he's intent on protecting,
possessing, and claiming me in every way—his little piece of purity.

But there is more to Max Butcher than the cold, cruel facade he wears
like armour. I know; I saw the broken boy inside him one day when we
were only children.

So, even as I stand in the shadows with him, as people get hurt…*as
people die…* I refuse to let him believe he's nothing more than a piece in
his family's corrupt empire.

There is good inside Max Butcher, and I refuse to let him live in the dark
forever.

Get book

Made in United States
North Haven, CT
17 May 2024

52601458R00082